TWIN PEAKS
OFFICE OF THE MAYOR

1 April 1991

As we always say to visitors to our town, "Greetings." I've spent eighty years here. Born here. Buried a brother here. And let me also add it's a wonderful place to eat.

So I take this opportunity to take pen in hand. Notwithstanding, I feel this kind can come in handy. ~~Whether~~ Whether you've lived here nine years or ninety. Or whether you just did.

My advice to those who visit is to get out. Get out and enjoy the weather and whatever.

I would like to pass on so many things to all of you. Not least of which would be the ability to look a total stranger in the eye and spout with a friendly air "Do you have that ten dollars you owe me?"

Thank You,

Best of Luck!

Mayor Milford

In Memory of Herbert F. Scherer, Sr.

Based upon characters and the fictitious town created by David Lynch and Mark Frost for the television series, *"Twin Peaks."*

Copyright © 1991 by Twin Peaks Productions, Inc. and **ACCESS**®PRESS. All rights reserved.

ISBN: 0-671-74399-6

Did you know that Twin Peaks ...

... consumes more doughnuts per capita than any city in the United States?

... is equidistant between Juneau, Alaska and Kayenta, Arizona?

... has one of the safest lumber mills in the country?

... has more dog and cat lovers than Tipton-on-Trent, England?

... displays more **Chinook** and **Kwakiutl** totem poles than the museum in Spokane?

... recently discovered our population is not 51,201?*

* the 1990 census revealed our present population is 5,120.1 **not** 51,201.

The following is an excerpt from the will of Andrew Packard, town father and patriarch of the Packard clan, one of Twin Peaks' two founding families, who was presumed dead after a boating accident on Black Lake, September 26, 1987.

Andrew Packard
1926-1987; and 1926-

Packard,A.   Notarization TP2783

"Item nine: To the good citizens of Twin Peaks,

In the event of my death, I, Andrew Packard, bequeath an unspecified sum to the town treasury, to be used solely and exclusively for the production and distribution of a book extolling and promulgating the many virtues and points of interest of our beloved community.

I also request that my good personal friend, Richard Saul Wurman, a man of hardy industry and responsible fiscal management, be made editor-in-chief of said book.

Having devoted the better part of my life to the betterment of our collective quality of life, I like to think of every last man, woman and child in Twin Peaks as a member of my family.

I fervently hope that this final gift to our town and its people, and the resulting document, will in time be seen as a lasting contribution to the continued development of our civic pride and sense of community, fostering understanding among us, communicating to others about us and helping all of us move towards a greater appreciation of God's great bounty of life which we all share here in Twin Peaks."

TABLE OF CONTENTS

TWIN PEAKS: A BRIEF HISTORY

The history of Twin Peaks is dominated by the lives of three great pioneer families. Two blessed by good fortune. One cursed by ill-tidings and disaster.

In 1888 Twin Peaks was little more than a small, rather untidy collection of refugees, trappers and thieves living in shacks along the shores of **Black Lake.** The **Wakahannawawak Trading Post**, later renamed **Thor's**, served the needs of this desolate group of individuals, dealing in furs, potables, and, some say, opium. However, the region's most valuable resource—its vast forest—remained untapped until **James Packard** and wife **Unguin** arrived two years later.

James Packard left a thriving family business in Boston to venture out into the great unknown. Educated at Harvard and Yale, James earned a reputation as a shrewd businessman, talented second tenor, and successful gambler. His wife **Unguin** dabbled in the mystic arts popular at the time. She was institutionalized briefly when she announced that her true home was located somewhere beyond the solar system in the mysterious Land of Bloon. Though Unguin spent the rest of her life in and out of several sanitariums, she did manage to successfully bear five healthy children.

James and **Unguin** originally intended to settle in Seattle. But sensing that his business opportunities would be better served in a less calcified environment, **James** and **Unguin** set out for the interior of the state in the spring of 1890.

Unguin Packard
1878-1974

Inspired by the thriving **Guilder Mill** in Tacoma, James purchased a huge tract of land upon arriving in Twin Peaks, and began work on what was to become the **Packard Mill**. **Unguin** formed an informal meeting club called Those of Bloon, and served as both chairperson and sergeant at arms for the next ten years until the club was disbanded during one of her frequent institutionalizations. Word of the Packard enterprise soon spread, and the riff-raff gathered along the shores of **Black**

Lake were replaced by lumberjacks and mill-workers drawn to the area by the promise of good work at a decent wage. The fact that the work was intolerable and the wages horrid seemed to have little effect on this optimistic band of class victims.

In 1891, **Rudolph** and **Pixie Martell** left their native St. Louis following a mysterious fire which destroyed their home. They migrated west, **Rudolph**'s head filled with stories of fabled gold mines and busy seaports, meaning to settle in San Francisco. But their mules died en route, and the **Martells** settled in Twin Peaks instead, continuing a long time family tradition: bad luck and worse timing.

Rudolph was a quiet man, contemplative, and prone to accidents like most of his ancestors. As a young man, he dabbled in painting and poetry, but after a rather serious bout with turpentine poisoning, it was determined that a life in business was more suited to his personal needs. **Pixie** was the daughter of a circus aerialist, forced to leave her family's performing troupe after causing an accident in St. Louis [*see*: *Great Circus Tragedies*. Odler Press, 1923). **Rudolph** met **Pixie** shortly thereafter and were wed.

Rudolph Martell was able to buy a sizable amount of land using what remained of his family's fortune. (His father was killed in a trolley accident. His mother perished due to a virulent form of scabies.) **Rudolph** soon began work on the **Martell Mill**. And though limited to the workers rejected by the **Packard Mill** — primarily Canadians and a visiting band of Icelandic lumberjacks — the new mill soon flourished. Twin Peaks was now dominated by twin timber dynasties. The **Packards** and the **Martells**.

Meanwhile, as homes sprung up along **Black Lake**, and the town of Twin Peaks began to take shape, **Orville Horne** and wife **Brulitha** arrived with plans for a general store to service the burgeoning community. **Orville Horne**, known as a "life-long bachelor", surprised his family by marrying **Brulitha**. The **Hornes** operated a

Rudolph Martell
1868-1931

TWAIN IN TWIN PEAKS

During his 1892 reading tour of the United States, the American writer, humorist and cynic Mark Twain cancelled a scheduled reading of his novel *Huckleberry Finn* at the Old Opera House when he emerged from the forests around Twin Peaks. "I feel as though I've been only a very few steps ahead of Death's hand the entire journey through that gloomy wood," he remarked. "The owls seemed to murmur my name as though my soul was already theirs."

LITTLE SCOTTIE

John Hanford, Twin Peaks' first mayor, was a man of high spirits who moderated his formidable sobriety with intermittent celebration. On one such occasion, July 4, 1891, in what is now the Roadhouse, he created our very own cocktail, the Little Scottie. Two parts bourbon, one part rye, with a dash of Drambuie and a twist of lime. Little Scotties still disappearin great numbers every weekend.

"Scottles," as we like to call them, are a local legend. Strained over cracked ice in a short glass and traditionally accompanied by cheese and crackers, they have been featured in *Spirits* magazine, discussed on the "Jerry Allen Show", and have even found their way into the pages of Jared Back's bestseller, *Backstop*.

It's hard to resist a well-made Scottie, but let us suggest moderation for the uninitiated. This is a sly dog with a big bite!

mercantile empire in Minnesota, and **Orville**, too impatient to wait to assume a leadership role in the dynasty, headed west to create one of his own.

Brulitha had earned a reputation as an excellent athlete and poetess, and later published *O Twin Peaks, My Land, My Home*, an epic poem often compared to the work of the region's poet laureate, **Hugo Boot**. [*see*: Boot. *Formidable or Fake*. Iambic Press, 1937.) **Horne**'s general store, known as **Horne's General Store**, competed for the town's business with **Thor's Trading Post** (formerly **Wakahannawawak**) until a suspicious fire leveled the Post, leaving **Horne's** as the region's only mercantile outlet. This virtual monopoly helped the general store to thrive, and after sustaining structural damage in the **Smallish Earthquake of 1905**, **Horne** rebuilt turning the relatively modest general store into what later became **Horne's Department Store**.

Not long after the turn of the century, the Packard-Martell timber rivalry entered its second generation. **Rudolph Martell** died an untimely death due to gangrene, and wife **Pixie** joined an Indian tribe in the southwest, leaving their son and heir, **Nealith Martell** to carry on. **Nealith** was known as both a dreamer and an invalid, and spent most of his life in bed. He married by mail order, and with wife **Bessie Spoon**, turned a wary eye toward the perpetuating of the family business.

But **Nealith** was not made for the rough and tumble world of timber. When a local inventor, **Crosby Truman**, offered him a patent on the revolutionary V-shaped flume, **Nealith** declined. **Truman** paid his next visit to the home of **Ezekial Packard**, a fabled domicile known as the **Blue Pine Lodge**.

Unlike **Nealith Martell**, **Ezekial Packard**, **James** and **Unguin**'s son, was born to business. Lacking even his father's passing interest in a world outside timber, **Ezekial** turned his powerful focus to the Packard lands and mill, seeking ways to both increase profits and gain competitive advantage over the remaining **Martells.** By purchasing the V-shaped flume outright, **Ezekial** was able to do exactly that. Soon the **Packard Mill** was nearly doubling the output of the Martell enterprise, and **Nealith**, confronted by a series of unlucky events and bad business decisions, was forced to sell his mill to the **Packards**. Later, **Nealith** died of food poisoning, and wife **Bessie** was struck by lightning, leaving a single heir, **Pete Martell**.

Freed of competition, **Ezekial** and his equally ambitious son, **Andrew**, were able to accelerate the family's hold on the region's resources. Later joined by sister **Catherine**, **Andrew Packard** built an empire whose name proudly resonates throughout Twin Peaks even today. Oddly enough, the last Martell, **Pete**, worked for the **Packards** as a lumberjack. And stranger still, he later married **Andrew**'s sister, **Catherine**.

Meanwhile, the **Horne** family continued to grow and prosper. **Orville Horne**'s son, **Ben**, carried on the family tradition by breaking ground for the **Great Northern Hotel** in 1927. The **Horne** hotel and department store, ably operated by Ben's son, **Ben Jr.**, formed the foundation for a family empire that soon stretched far beyond the borders of Twin Peaks.

With **Andrew Packard**'s disappearance in 1988, the last of the second generation pioneers was lost to us. But the names **Packard**, **Horne**, and to a lesser extent, **Martell**, still ring proudly through the history of Twin Peaks. That before us, and that which is to come.

JOSIE PACKARD—**Virgo,** Josie Packard hails from Hong Kong, though Twin Peaks has provided her more adventure than she ever imagined possible, or probable. As the youngest female executive and owner of the Packard Mill, the wife of lately-reappearing Andrew Packard is keenly self-motivated. Born September 2, 1962, Josie admits to troubling thoughts and occasional doubts about the men in her life.

BESTS: "The sound of the water, White Tail roaring, when I feel like a rushing torrent-falling." Also, the Blue Pine Lodge "when Pete is there to make me laugh" and travel to mysterious places.

WILDE IN TWIN PEAKS

Oscar Wilde **made a detour from his planned itinerary in order to visit Twin Peaks in 1902.** Traveling up the coast from San Francisco to Seattle by steamer and from Seattle to Twin Peaks by mule, Wilde quipped upon his return, "Who ever met a lumberjack they didn't like?"

THE OLD OPERA HOUSE

BENJAMIN "Ben" HORNE
—Born August 4, 1940. In
a world lacking in virility
and in need of a hero, Twin
Peaks is honored to have
Ben Horne as one of its
most prominent citizens. A
Leo, this former President
of SAE at Stanford University—where his nickname
was "Peacock"—pursues
with gusto everything life
offers. A firm believer in
cross-cultural relations
and the restorative power
of song, he supports joint
U.S.-Canadian enterprises
and often travels north in
pursuit of things.

BESTS: "Twin Peaks'
incredible potential, far-
sighted citizens, and location, location, location."

Two blocks south of County Road J on Route 21 you will see where the first **Opera House** was built in 1882. Inaugurating it was the divine **Sarah Bernhardt** in *Camille* [see page 23]. Destroyed by the **Terrible Fire of 1896**, it was rebuilt in 1916 for the tenor **Enrico Caruso** who got lost and missed the show. In 1918, with better directions, he sang a concert of **James Packard**'s favorites.

Progress altered the **Opera House** in 1925 when the old stage and hemp flylines disappeared behind Twin Peaks' first Silver Screen on which was shown **Charlie Chaplin**'s *The Gold Rush* on a double bill with *The Battleship Potemkin* of **Sergei Eisenstein** who was a Russian.

Abandoned four decades later, it remained vacant until 1969 when the rock group **Guess Who** caused such a tumult the Town Council banned rock concerts in Twin Peaks unless written assurances were received that the performers would behave properly.

"Ben" Horne restored the theatre's interior and exterior in 1982 according to the original architect's design and citizens of Twin Peaks are once again going to the movies! 555-FILM.

Caruso in Twin Peaks

The famous tenor sang at the **New Opera House** in 1918 (which replaced the Old **Opera House** that burned to the ground in the Fire of 1896) by singing arias from *Rigoletto*, *La Boheme*, *Tosca*, *Pagliacci* and several other of **James Packard**'s favorites. **Mr. Caruso**'s accompanist fell ill prior to the concert and James' daughter, **Mavis**, had the honor of accompanying the world-famous tenor. Known as an avid gastronome, **Mr. Caruso** took with him from the burgeoning community an authentic Snoqualmie Indian war bonnet as well as the recipe for Huckleberry pie, admitting, "Never again can I conclude a meal with a sweet like *dolce torinese* after that delicious Huckleberry pie."

THE VERSATILE HUCKLE-BERRY

Huckleberries (***Vaccinium membranaceum***) were a vital food source for the Flathead **and other tribes. In midsummer they were gathered and spread out on hides to dry. Mashed into a thick pulp, they were patted into cakes and set in the sunlight on rocks until they dried. Also popular was** Huckleberry **soup in which the berries were boiled with roots such as wild carrot or Camas added as thickener or sweetener. It took a homemaker from back east,** Belinda Bondace, **to acquaint the natives with Huckleberry pie.**

FIRST INHABITANTS

It is generally accepted that the first humans in the northwest migrated from Asia during the final stages of the Quaternary Glacial Epoch when dropping sea levels allowed the **Siber** (as in 'Siberian') people to forage over a land bridge connecting the two continents. A natural corridor formed by the receding Laurentian Ice Shield funnelled, as it were, these tribes down to present-day Alberta, British Columbia, Washington, Idaho and Oregon. From there they spread west to the Pacific Coast. Abundant timber, freshwater fish, deer, otter and beaver, as well as a richness of wild berries provided the means by which these tribes survived and prospered. Those who tired of the thick, gloomy forests and the disturbing sounds of the owls continued south to present-day Palm Springs and Phoenix. The remaining tribes, however, moved through the forests and formed 'families' such as the **Snoqualmie**, **Umpqua**, **Methow**, **Cayuse**, **Yakima**, **Spokan**, **Flathead** and **Nez Perce**. Pinpointing a precise date for this migration is difficult, but it is likely these immigrants from Asia appeared in the rich forests of Washington around 25,000 years ago.

Some Yakima carvings, like the danger mask above, play an important role in story telling and in the passing on of fables from one generation to the next.

Our knowledge of the early history of these settlers is imperfect because of a lack of pottery fragments, dur to their reliance on perishable materials such as wood and leaves, and because some of them developed paranoid tendencies, becoming excessively secretive and morbid. [*see*: Billings, T. *The Function of Neurosis in Snoqualmie Culture.* TP Press, 1932.]

Wall totem, believed to have been carved in honor of the 'Grandmother of Salmon,' a minor presence in Snoqualmie Indian lore.

As is true of families throughout history, these Northwest tribes created distinguishing traditions. One trait shared by all, if we can believe reports from the first white explorers who met them, was an attitude toward possessions which Europeans found bizarre. These patriarchal societies of Amerindians seemed to have a peculiar regard for their canoes, hides, weapons, heraldic crests, slaves and little stones they called 'pebbles' which they used to pitch at people considered stupid or too short. In fact, the word *potlatch* (a feast of generosity, or gift) was bequeathed to our language from the Nootka tribe from their expression *potshatl* or 'giving'. At this religious ceremony, the host would honor his guests by giving his wealth away to them or actually destroying it. **Angus MacDowell** wrote a typically biased account of *potlatch* or *potshatl* in an 1817 diary entry: "(I) couldn't believe my eyes. The host actually cut himself up, and as guests left they took with them a hand or toe or thigh of their host. I tell you, this potlatch stuff is very wasteful and I was shamed by it. Since most of what is given away looked to me like junk, I wonder why it is not recycled."

Northwest Indian "pebbles" discovered near present-day intersection of Sparkwood and Falls Avenue.

It was (and sadly still is) unfortunate the anglo mind did not comprehend the religious significance of these traditions and continually misrepresented them. A *potshatl*, in particular, represented the Amerindians' disinterest in 'possessions.' Settlers were always asking them who owned the land, a question the original Americans simply did not understand because the idea of ownership was—the irony is appropriate—foreign to them.

Warfare and raiding were a way of life, though the weapons employed by these tribes were hardly sophisticated, and most of the fatalities were caused by skull laceration and severe brain trauma. A few of the tribes actually formed Secret Societies of Cannibalism. Most vicious were the **Snoqualmie, Kwakiutl** and **Circulars** [see pages 64, 101].

BUILDING A CANOE

The Paper Birch has been a friend to Amerindians and beavers for centuries. While the long-haired, toothy rodent prefers its inner bark, the outer layers of this tree were employed by Indians to make the skin of their canoes. They began with a skeletal structure of the pliant White Cedar. Over this, sheets of Paper Birch bark were stitched together, then sealed with pine or balsam resin.

13

Chinook legends describe the appearance long ago of an ancestress of the frog clan. They tell of a house, floating in the middle of a lake. On the house sits a woman, her knees, breasts, eyebrows and the backs of her hands covered with flying frogs. Ever since that time, the flying frog has been viewed as a special crest.

The Indians were very interested in commerce and when they were not clubbing one another into insensibility they formed hubs such as the Dalles Fishing Center on the Columbia River. There, **Chinook** tribes traded and passed on hunting and fishing tips to the **Plateau Indians** through the use of what became known as the **Chinook Jargon**, a language eventually used throughout the region by Indians and white men.

It is only within the most recent decades of this country's history that Amerindian culture has begun to be understood and valued by the foreign cultures that engulfed but never embraced it.

An early resident of the area…

…now resides in the County Museum.

FIRST EXPLORERS

The first European of record to appear on the northwest coast was **Juan Rodriguez Cabrillo** who pulled into present day **Puget Sound** in 1542 to ask directions. Francis Drake (not yet a 'Sir') slid into the bay some thirty years later and, ignorant of Juan or, more likely, anti-Spanish, named the land **Nova Albion**, claiming it for **Elizabeth I**. It took the Russians a little longer to show up; in 1741, **Vitus Behring** and **Peter Cherikof** put in an appearance. Of course, the Bering Straits between Russia and Alaska are named for **Vitus**, a fact that has caused no little irritation to the **Chinook**

Indians prompting them to savagely slaughter untold boatloads of fur-seeking Russias until **Ivan Pritikoff**, in 1795, concluded the Treaty of Vladivostok (which became the title of an unfinished novel by **Pushkin** and a forgotten opera by **Mussorgsky**) which gave the **Chinook** the right to refer to the icy winds that blow out of the north as a "chinook."

Explorers approaching the northwest overland from the east did not arrive until the latter half of the 18th century. They came for two reasons: 1) because of a rodent, and 2) a European fashion craze.

French and English hatters had discovered the pelts of a tree-eating animal called the beaver made superb felt and the **beaver hat** became all the rage, inspiring hundreds of Frenchmen to seek their fortunes among the waterways and forests of the new world. As beaver were killed off in one area, these *coureurs de bois* pursued them further into the unexplored region. They would refer to the animal as having "split" when it became extinct in one area. Hence, the term **split beaver**.

In 1670 the King of England granted a Royal Charter to the **Hudson Bay Company**, (the company's shield is shown above) allowing them to exploit virtually the entire continent.

The first white man of record to reach the Pacific northwest overland in 1793 was **Alexander MacKenzie**. From the new country called America, John Jacob Astor sent out his agents to subdue the mighty beaver after **Lewis and Clark** opened a path through the wilderness to the Pacific in 1804-5.

15

Twin Peaks: Early Fame

Merriwether Lewis **and** William Clark**, guided by the Shoshone** Sacagawea, became internationally famous for navigating a path across North America to the Pacific Coast. In a diary entry of June 13, 1805, Lewis wrote that he saw "two mountains of a singular appearance and more like ramparts of high fortification than works of nature."

Lewis must have been refering to Twin Peaks! It's been postulated that shortly after leaving the area of present-day Missoula, the expedition made a strange detour to the north as shown on this map.

Sometime in the late 18th or early 19th century (August 10th, 1803 has been suggested), one **Dominick Renault** apparently struggled to the shores of **Black Lake** in the northeast corner of present-day Washington. Having set out from Montreal more than a year earlier to discover the **Northwest Passage**, **Renault** gave up his dream when tribe after tribe of Indians laughed in his face. After his career as a stand-up comic in Chilliwack fizzled, Dominick fled south in despair of his life. Clues to his progress are few, most a matter of legend [*see*: Targaski, E. *French Explorers: Enigmas in Fur*. Paris and London: The Overseas Press, 1917.], but we know he appeared on the shore of **Black Lake** and soon established a trading post half a mile above **White Tail Falls**.

Diary fragments indicate **Renault** was a gloomy man, given to extended and severe depressions from which he emerged apparently believing he'd been talking with animals. A fragment of his trading post still exists, though no one knows what became of **Renault**. Most likely, as **Targaski** suggests, he mated with owls, his anguished voice becoming a part of them in the endless and misty forests.

Dominick Renault
1775-1855

COUNTY MUSEUM

Not to be missed when you're visiting Twin Peaks, the **County Museum** on Route 21 just south of town is a warehouse of information and sights relating to Twin Peaks' magnificent past and promising future.

Overseen by **Elsa Eisenbuch** and curator **Milford Mertz**, the museum boasts a permanent collection of early Amerindian artifacts, replete with dioramas of Indian villages and early finishing techniques. Yet the museum is also on the cutting edge of the contemporary art world. In March 1989 they had on loan an exhibition of **Robert Mapplethorpe** photographs, so far-seeing is this museum and its Board. Most visitors, however, are drawn to the flora and fauna exhibits cribbed from the New York City Museum of Natural History. The dead and stuffed animals are surprisingly life-like and safety is ensured because they are behind glass.

Open from May to the end of September, 11:00AM to 3:00PM weekdays and 1:00PM to 4:00PM on Saturday. Call ahead and Elsa will arrange a tour for you (German translator provided free of charge). A donation of $1.50 is suggested but not mandatory, though Elsa disagrees. Coffee is always available, but not always fresh. On Route 21, southwest of Twin Peaks in Lower Town. 555-8800.

Early artifact in County Museum.

The original craftsman-ship of the totem pole is unknown. Its origins were traced back to Horne's General Store. Best recollection has it looking very similar to the one that was in Thor's Trading Post prior to the fire.

17

THE PACKARD MILL

Packard Sawmill

CATHERINE MARTELL see Packard—**Born November 4, 1940 under Scorpio as well as a half moon, and the lifeless gaze of several stuffed animals murdered by her sporting father, Catherine graduated from our high school with a remarkable command of French, Japanese and the Kama Sutra.**

BESTS: Twin Peaks generally quiescent population, "Elvis Presley" and, sometimes, the Horne.

**Daisy Packard
1894-1960**

Oregon Historical Society, #ORHI 86112

THE PACKARD MILL THEN

The **Packard Mill** was founded in 1890. **James Packard** had come here that year from Boston. A clumsy but alert young man, he soon recognized that his fortune lay in **Douglas Fir.**

The original mill was built on two acres next to the **Black Lake Falls** and employed only eight men. After a short altercation with the **Kwakiutl Indians** (resolved when James agreed to trade cough drops in exchange for the land), James and his crew chopped down a few dozen trees, turned them into board, and literally built the mill around themselves. The big saw (its blades were six feet in diameter) originally drew its power directly from the rushing water above the falls.

James Packard fathered five children, four girls (**Daisy, Addy, Roslyn** and **Mavis**) and one boy, **Ezekial**. Under Ezekial's direction, the family business was to become a thriving cornerstone of the county's economy. In 1922 he razed the old mill and erected a much larger structure on the same site, covering 25 acres and requiring more than six million board feet of lumber. By 1924, the **Packard Mill** employed nearly 100 people in cutting, floating, sawing, shipping, and maintaining the plant.

At the outbreak of the **Second World War**, management of the mill passed temporarily to **Daisy Packard**, who, by the end of the war, was to prove herself a formidable businesswoman.

By 1945, **Daisy** was known all over the state as an innovative business leader. New technologies that she introduced included **mechanical barkers** (machines that stripped the bark from the logs in a fraction of the time required by manual labor), the **skyhook cable car** to fly the lumber down from the high ridges, and the **wigwam burner** used to dispose of the mill's debris.

In 1948, at the age of twenty-two, Ezekial's son, **Andrew**, came into his own and took over management of the mill. Andrew completed the work his aunt had started, modernizing the actual log cutting with the introduction of the chain saw in the early '50s. By 1972, he had computerized the plant's machinery, increasing production by more than 25 percent.

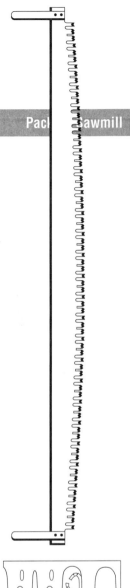

Packard Sawmill

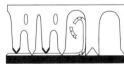

Crosscut saw and detail

The skyhook cable car, strung between steep ridges, 'flew' lumber down to makeshift railways for transportation to the mill.

For the next sixteen years, the **Packard Mill** continued to prosper, reaching peak production in 1988.

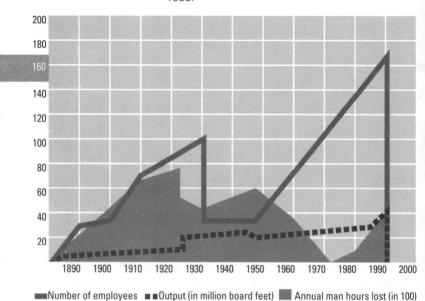

■■Number of employees ■ ■Output (in million board feet) ■ Annual man hours lost (in 100)

THE PACKARD MILL NOW

As the largest employer in Twin Peaks, the **Packard Mill** is dedicated to preserving and promulgating community standards, health and high employment. With one of the largest and most stable mill rolls in the state, management eagerly accepts its responsibility for integrity and far-sightedness. For example, as an incentive to on-the-job safety, the company sponsors a barbecue to reward the workers when a quarter has passed without accident or injury. And the department managers do the cooking! It's been more effective than tacking up safety posters on the walls and the last barbecue in 1972 is still being talked about.

Upgraded more often than most mills, machinery at **Packard Mill** begins with the debarkers, a 43 inch Nicholson and a Schurman rosser head, both heavily mortgaged but worth it. After a six foot Salem mill, the lines feed into a Gunnarson resaw, a Schurman four-saw selective edger and a 32 foot Albany trimmer, all kept shipshape by Plant Boss **Arnie Moulton**. "Safety is paramount, after profit and management perks," says Arnie. "But it's often over-valued. Reality is the name of the . . . whatchamacallit."

Putting out nearly 150,000 board feet a day, the mill is in production four days a week because the employees prefer it that way and management easily caves in. The **log inventory** is between four and five million board feet. All logs are kept in dry storage until they are distributed across the United States or exported to Australia, New Zealand and Japan. (Though very few logs, perhaps two or three at most and some plywood and a little pulp, though not much.)

As a cutting mill, the **Packard Mill** focuses on maximizing higher-value grades and that means a lot of interaction between the workers and the wood. **Wood Mistress**, **Helga Brogger** explains, "Misunderstandings arise and intimacies occur but the weekly grading classes are helpful in this regard."

Production over the past five years is up 34% without much capital reinvestment, but the recent tragic and calamitous fire that started in the drying shed will offer to our community the very sort of challenge it relishes. Insurers are suggesting arson but Manager of holding and drying, **Bill Grose**, shakes his head. "Drying's tricky stuff," Bill says, seraphically, "and, being a Theosophist, tricky stuff is, well, it's a toss-up how that fire started but it could have. It could have."

Twin Peaks looks forward with optimism and courage to rebuilding the **Packard Mill** and once again exporting wood to the world!

The mill is located on Sparkwood Rd. and tours available on Tuesday and Thursday between 10:00AM and 4:00PM, each hour on the hour. Now that the mill's burned to soot, though, the tours are likely to discontinue. Call the **Twin Peaks Chamber of Commerce**, to check.

BERNHARDT'S BONER

Known as the era's most compelling actress, the divine Sarah Bernhardt **inaugurated Twin Peaks' first** Opera House **in 1882. Unbeknownst to most of her admirers, the divine** Sarah **suffered an accident that left her with only one good leg. Her excellence enabled her to disguise that one leg was made of wood! While in Twin Peaks, the wooden leg was damaged one morning as the spiritually-minded actress was enacting her Paean to Aurora below the** Packard Mill **on the shore of** Black Lake. **Always gallant, Mr.** Packard **intervened and offered to fashion a new leg of durable and attractive** Douglas Fir. **No one knows if she ever employed it but Mr.** Packard **insisted she was very generous with her thanks.**

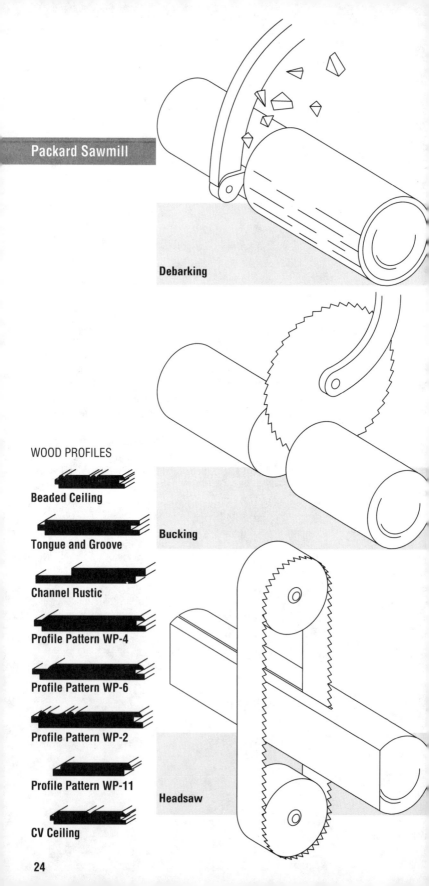

Debarking

Bucking

WOOD PROFILES

Beaded Ceiling

Tongue and Groove

Channel Rustic

Profile Pattern WP-4

Profile Pattern WP-6

Profile Pattern WP-2

Profile Pattern WP-11

CV Ceiling

Headsaw

esaws

de edging

imming

ished board

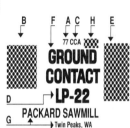

```
    B      F  A C  H        E
    ↓      ↓  ↓ ↓  ↓        ↓
                77 CCA
           GROUND
           CONTACT
D          → LP-22
   G   PACKARD SAWMILL
        → Twin Peaks, WA
```

A Year of treatment

B Trademark of building-
   code-approved quality
   control agency

C The preservative used
   for treatment

D Preservative retention
   level and/or the quality
   control agency
   procedure indication

E Trademark of agency
   supervising the treating
   plant

F Proper exposure
   conditions

G Treating company and
   plant location

H DRY or DKAT proce-
   dures, if applicable

25

Whittlers should have at least seven fingers.

THE JOYS OF WHITTLING

An unfortunate but **common misperception** about whittlers is that they are dumb. This is not true. They tend to be slow and occasionally a good deal duller than their knife-blades, true enough, but stupidity is not characteristic of them as a group.

This fallacy behind us, the **joys of whittling** are being discovered daily by dozens of adults and children. After all, it is inexpensive, and you need only a good pocketknife, a piece of wood and two hands with ten fingers (seven are considered a minimum requirement). Moreover, a whittler's workshop is limitless.

Whittling is, basically, carving a piece of wood with a knife. In fact, in **Europe** whittling is called 'carving a piece of wood with a knife.' It is never referred to as 'whittling.' Where the term comes from is shrouded in mystery, which is why whittlers are considered so enigmatic.

Here are a few pointers:

1 Use a good, **sharp knife**. This will facilitate working the wood as well as prevent accidents and a need for expensive major medical plans. A **two-bladed, steel pocketknife** is a good starter, though as you improve you'll want to add a short-bladed sloyd knife, a small skew knife and a band saw to your collection.

The big ugly wood bear is an example of the joys of whittling gone astray.

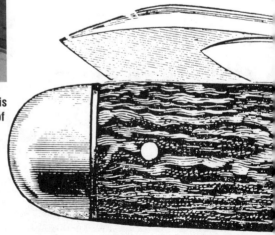

Cooper's Whistle

2 A **whetstone** or **oilstone** is indispensable in holding an edge to the knifeblade. Remember, a dull blade gathers moss and the likelihood of injury, not to mention infection, is only increased with one. A sharp blade cuts clean, whether in wood or flesh.

3 Select a **softwood** to whittle. Oak and ash are just going to mess you up and piss you off. **Basswood** is good, both seasoned and green, especially if you can't find white pine. But select a non-resinous wood.

4 Finally, a good supply of **cloth band-aids** is worthwhile. More experienced whittlers are also skilled in the use of the tourniquet and will have a selection of hemostats in their kits.

Whittling is a fad whose time has come and in Twin Peaks we're on the cutting edge. So, ***ENJOY!***

DALE BARTHOLOMEW "Coop" COOPER—**Born April 19, 1954. An FBI Agent and Aries, might well have been a magician or mystic had he not scored a perfect 100 on his Eagle Scout marksmanship test, after which his thinking took a decidedly 'legalistic' turn. Unable to escape the memory of a tragic incident in his recent past,** Coop **likes jelly doughnuts and a good cup of Joe.**

BESTS: "The whole remarkable town, the whole thing; I mean all of it." Also, the Theosophist Society.

Advertisement

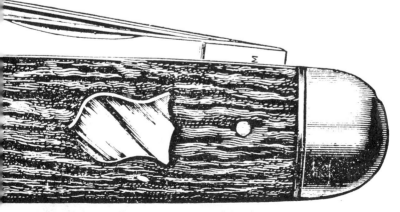

Wood Cutting Patterns

Through and through

True radiant

Billet

Plain

Board and structure

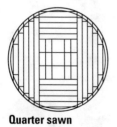

Quarter sawn

THE WOOD MISTRESS

The **Packard Mill** prides itself on a stable employee roll and no worker exemplifies stability and longevity more than **Wood Mistress Helga Brogger**.

Sitting in her chair on a thick Naugahyde pillow and expertly eyeing the great timbers as they enter the mill, **Helga** discerns in an instant a log's fate—whether it is soft and knotted for pulp, strong and hard for structural use, or even-grained and knot-free for veneer. Wielding a four foot stick tipped with chalk, the mill's highest paid worker flicks her wrist and the decision is made. "Mix 'n' match, " she sneers at pulp. "Trusses," she giggles and blushes at structural pieces. Veneer logs bring forth a bright and sassy, "Hi, handsome!"

In **Helga**'s case, the expert eye of **Wood Mistress** is not learned; it was bequeathed by previous generations of **Brogger** women. "My mother and grandmother, both knew a good piece when they saw it. Just like me. It runs in the family; women of vision, the backbone of Twin Peaks."

Married to **Bjorn Brogger**, former director of Meals on Wheels, **Helga** hasn't missed a day at work, say fans. When double pneumonia caused the loss of one lung, legend has it **Helga** had it removed on the weekend and was back in her chair on Monday.

Is it true she's 72 years old? "I'll admit to being over 50," **Helga** says, then whoops with merry laughter. "Here in Twin Peaks we tell tales that are like **Douglas Fir** trees—pretty tall."

TWIN PEAKS FLORA

The forests, rivers, lakes and mountains around Twin Peaks are a nature lover's bonanza. Residents of the town disappear for days at a time (some have disappeared forever) to lose themselves in the riot of wilderness.

Leaving Lower Town as sunlight touches the tips of **Sparkwood** and **Blue** mountains and proceeding east into **Ghostwood National Forest**, one cannot help but be struck by the variety of flora, as well as low-hanging branches if you're not alert. On these lower elevations, or *plateaus,* deciduous (leaf-bearing) trees such as **Oregon White Oak**, **Rocky Mountain Maple** and **Paper Birch** [see Box below] proliferate in rich soil. In North America, the **Paper Birch** is one of the most widely distributed trees and often the first specie to establish itself in fire-ravaged areas, which is why they are so abundant around Twin Peaks; the **Smallish Earthquake of 1905** and ensuing fire devastated thousands of acres.

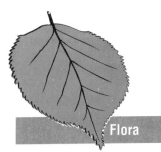

Paper Birch leaf

LAWRENCE "Doc" JACOBY—**Born January 30, 1934. Abjuring the Logical Positivist school of philosophy by turning instead to Spiderman and the *National Enquirer* while growing up in Hawaii, Aquarian "Doc" balances the right and left sides of his brain by wearing rose and aqua colored glasses.**

Ferns and Flowers

A glance at your feet will reveal to the practiced eye **Western Sword Fern,** an erect frond, bristle-toothed with alternating leaflets.

BESTS: The awesome number of dysfunctional families in Twin Peaks and "my mailman, who argues with each envelope, analyzes the suitability of the stamp, a real case."

Specimens of the **Snow Plant** are collected by sometime naturalist Dr. Jacoby. Found in deep forest humus, this is a leafless plant, 4 to 12 inches tall, that is fleshy with leaf-like scales. It is a deep red, resembling an elongated heart or discarded chunk of bloody meat. Whoever named the snow plant obviously had a finely honed sense of irony.

Snoqualmie **legend tells of a tribesman who came upon a wounded mountain lion and removed an arrow from its thigh. Years later when the animal died, it turned into a Lily. Shortly after, the**

Flora

Indian who befriended the lion died, and lilies spread all over the land in search of their friend.

As the deciduous trees give way to mountain meadow, observe the **Yellow Lupines** and **Leopard Lilies**. The former is potentially poisonous if large quantities are eaten and is often confused with the **False Lupine** (which has flowers arranged in groups of three, not four and five like the genuine article). The **Leopard Lily** grows from two to eight feet in height. Its red-orange flowers with maroon spots are unmistakable and the bell-shaped petals curl like a pouting lower lip.

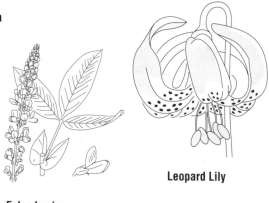

Leopard Lily

False Lupine

Yellow Lupine

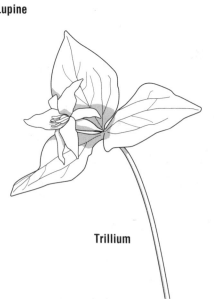

Trillium

Giant Red Paintbrush

Other ferns and flowers you will see are **Trillum**, **Deer Fern**, **Vanilla Leaf** and **Giant Red Paintbrush**, identified by its tuft of red spines atop a one to three foot stalk in mountain meadows and near stream banks.

Pines and Firs

Moving to higher ground, the air cools, feels clean and crisp except when you're socked in by gray clouds and getting rained on. But when the sun shines and birds sing, you're soon inspired by the appearance of vast pine forests stretching to the horizon.

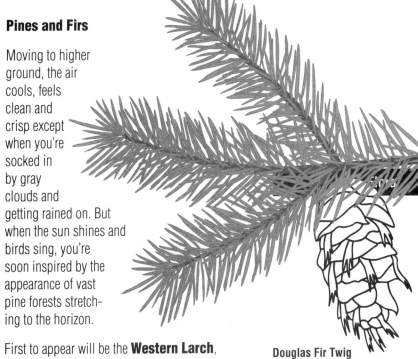

Douglas Fir Twig

First to appear will be the **Western Larch**, **Mountain** and **Western Hemlock** and **Ponderosa Pine**. Though a conifer (cone-bearing and 'needled'), the **Larch** is the only needled tree that loses its 'leaves' in late autumn and remains bare all winter. Mice, chipmunk and birds feed on its seeds. Providing excellent cover for the **Blue Grouse** (a 16"-19" bird that produces loud, booming noises by using air sacs on the sides of its throat and is often admonished by its neighbors to shut up) is the **Mountain Hemlock** that may live for four and five centuries, much like its close relative, the **Western Hemlock**, though the latter is a tall but shallow-rooted tree easily toppled by heavy snows and wind. The gray-black bark of both trees is rich in tannin [see page 36].

The **Ponderosa Pine** is a true pine tree, as tall as 180 feet and distributed over much of the Western U.S. Unlike the flat, short-needled hemlocks and cedars, its clusters of three (or three and two) blue-green needles as well as its scaly, plated brownish-orange bark make it easy to identify. A cub of this fragrant wood is seen at all times in the arms of the Log Lady.

Growing in dense thickets in the pine forests you will note the **Saskatoon Serviceberry**. Their fleshy fruits were eaten raw or cooked and made

The above Ponderosa Pine log was a gift to Lanterman (The Log Lady) on her wedding night from her late husband who was a fire fighter.

Saskatoon Serviceberry

into jams by Indians. No one knows how this plant came by its helpful and beguiling name, although **Helga Brogger** says she knows but won't tell.

Soon, you approach the most majestic trees of the area around Twin Peaks—**the Douglas Fir**—with their thick, deeply furrowed bark. The wood of these 800 to 1,000 year old trees is some of the finest in the world and used in construction for structural supports in bridges and docks and railroad trestles. Because the wood does not warp it is excellent for interior finishes and plywood. Found in predominantly 'pure' stands, it creates superb windbreaks while providing cover for many animals, especially the **Great Horned** and **Pygmy Owls**.

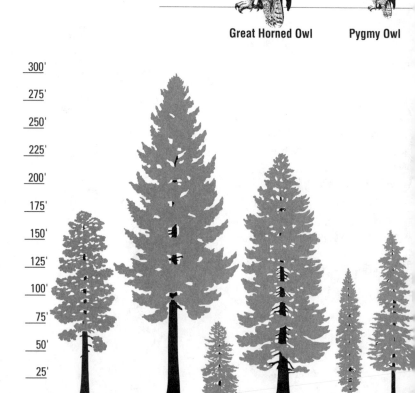

Great Horned Owl   Pygmy Owl

300'
275'
250'
225'
200'
175'
150'
125'
100'
75'
50'
25'
0

Ponderosa Pine   Douglas Fir   White Spruce   Western Red Cedar   Western White Pine   Western Hemlock

Other Flora

Western Red Cedar - Grows on lower mountain slopes and open valleys in pure, dense stands or with **Douglas Firs**. Lives up to 500 years. Five to nine lobes per leaf. Good hardwood for furniture and cabinets. Acorns important to deer, bear, squirrels and woodpeckers. Used by Indians for totem poles.

Red Alder - Found among **Douglas Fir**. Sixty to eighty year life span. Improves fertility of soils. Good hardwood for inexpensive furniture, for smoking meats and wood-carving.

Mountain Alder - Good for firewood and little else.

Quaking Aspen - Wide distribution in U.S. 500 species of animals *and* plants use them—from bear and elk to fungi. **Favorite food of the beaver!!!** Primarily for paper products; weak wood.

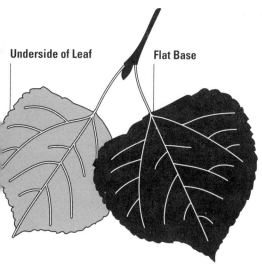

Underside of Leaf   Flat Base

THE LOG LADY—**Born under achingly clear and brilliant skies on an unknown date, The Log Lady is a self-proclaimed Libra and graduate of Twin Peaks High School. After further matriculation at Evergreen State University as a Forestry and Wildlife Management major, she met a fire fighter and the rest is history. When not teaching Fire Prevention and ballroom dancing, The Log Lady ministers to the sick and the sick at heart. "My strength,' she explains, "is in my forearms."**

Pacific Dogwood - IMPORTANT!!! It is similar to **Flowering Dogwood** except its flowers are surrounded by five bracts rather than four (feel better now?). Red and orange berries provide food for quail, hermit thrushes, bandtailed pigeons and vireos.

Rocky Mountain Maple - In sheltered canyons, ravines and moist slopes. Good hardwood but trees too small for commercial use. Great for campfires and wood stoves.

BESTS: Bear Claws and broccoli, long walks in the woods and listening to the mysterious knowledge of her log. Also, Glastonberry Grove.

33

Moss

While marveling at the magnificent landscape on your nature tour, don't forget to look down every now and again. This will not only enable you to avoid tripping over things and possibly injuring yourself, but also to see something Twin Peaks has in abundance: moss.

The first green plant to develop in the process of evolution (Creationists place it on the 6th Day), these colorful and furry patches of bryophyton make wonderful, cuddly gifts for pre-schoolers and shut-ins, though they should not be eaten. Used by **Kwakiutl** medicine men to heal wounds and tell time, moss is found most often on the north sides of trees and rocks, something to keep in mind if you're lost without a compass. In fact, the earliest reference to these green rugs that are not unlike some brands of indoor/outdoor carpeting is found in **Gaston Leroux**'s diary of May 1787. Apparently lost, the French trapper and pedophile wrote: "I carry a supply of moss in my pack to tell me which way I'm going. It makes for inestimably fine company and never interrupts, though it must be disciplined from time to time." The diary was found with the remains of **Leroux**'s bones not far from **Owl Cave**, around which moss is abundant.

Naomi Swart's recipe for moss stew is really something, though the stew itself isn't.

Flora

Devil's Club
Growing at or near the base of many Hemlocks **is the** Devil's Club, **an 8' tall wild plant with sprigs of red berries among Maple-like leaves. It is** not to be touched! **Yellow spines bristle from its stalk and barbs on stems and the undersides of its leaves pierce the skin like porcupine quills.** Dominick Renault **ignorantly grabbed one to taste its berries when he came upon** Black Lake **in the late 18th century. Only two** Great Horned Owls **overheard his exclamations of gutter-French but they were memorable enough to have been passed down through successive generations of these immense and graceful birds.**

Cladonia peaksidata

Cladonia duoflorica

Cetraria dobbiata

Cetraria frostifera

Poison Ivy

After you have sleuthed among trees, flowers and fronds for those elusive patches of moss and returned home with an abundant supply for future birthdays and holidays [see the TPCC pamphlet, *Keeping Moss Moist*], you may notice after three or four days the spreading of an itchy rash over parts of your body. Don't be too alarmed; you've had an encounter with another plant found growing wild and rampant around Twin Peaks: **Poison Ivy**. While it is easily identified by its three dark green,

*Leaves of three...
Let them be!*

shiny oval leaves one to two inches long growing on each branch of the plant, even the most knowledgeable naturalist will pick up a case now and then. Caused by oil from the plant coming into contact with your skin, the rash can be efficaciously treated by applying readily available lotions found at our drugstore. **Mort Zafkee** says, "Really severe cases should be swabbed with boiling lye and vigorously attacked with steel wool or a metal brush. Total immersion of the affected areas in really hot grease or removing the agonized limb with a band saw will also stop the itching." **Doc Hayward** says, with a wink, "Mort's a kidder. But if it's the itching you want to stop, he's got a point." Intimate contact with others is discouraged while the rash persists. **The Poison Ivy Epidemic of 1818** carried off two dozen lusty pioneers and trappers before the elk and caribou populations closed ranks and the dread rash faded away.

This innocent and not unattractive little plant can pack a wallop, so know what it looks like and treat it with respect.

TOMMY "the Hawk" HILL —Born September 16, 1950. A Virgo, Hawk is a unique combination of pragmatist and mystic. Son of a Zuni Shaman, he admits to being intolerant of those who would destroy the earth's beauty and allows that he did, indeed, run the wrong way in that final game of the '68 season.

BESTS: Timber games, grass between your toes and cool, clear water.

Tanned Hides

While the eastern **Hemlock** forests were virtually decimated by the tanning industry in the mid-nineteenth century, western forests escaped the wholesale elimination of these majestic trees, although several tanning companies operated on the **Columbia River**. South of Twin Peaks on the banks of the **Rattail River**, the **Ladoux Tannery** began operations in 1892. Hides from San Francisco and Seattle were brought overland or upriver to the tannery because it was more economical to transport hides than **Hemlock** bark. Also, the stench of a tannery was more easily tolerated in a wilderness than an already over-ripe metropolis.

The bark of the Hemlock tree is rich with **tannin** which, when heated in water, releases a chemical enzyme particularly useful in softening hides.

The trees were felled, and their branches hacked off with axes. At that point, a long-handled tool called a **spud** was employed; the men who wielded them called **spudders**. A curved and razor-sharp blade slide between the bark of the tree and its wood. Agitating and slicing pried the bark away. What remained of the tree was shamefully left to rot (though around Twin Peaks an army of under-achievers known as **whittlers** scavenged **Hemlock** trees from which they created large but extremely graceful statues that played a significant role in the whittlers' lurid *tableaux vivant* on Saturday nights).

Heated and mulched in immense oak vats, the bark eventually dissolved. It was then transferred to smaller cast iron 'tubs' into which the hides were introduced and boiled .

Nothing remains to tell us precisely where the **Ladoux Tannery** stood on the **Rattail River**. Only **Agnes Turnquist**'s diary alludes to its existence in a July 19, 1893 entry; "That tannery is a scourge on the land. Daddy allows it smells terrible and mother agrees, but Arvid and me say it stinks like s—t."

Flora

Types of Spuds

1

2

3

4

5

1 **Made from auto spring**
2 **Heinback spud**
3 **Spoon-shaped spud**
4 **Narrow spud for hardwoods**
5 **Cedar spud**

THE TWIN PEAKS FLOWER: A PINE CONE

A simple pine cone to some, but not to us. To firs, hemlocks, pines and other conifers know as gymnosperms this item is the basic goods, the means of reproduction. Most trees will drop the whole cone to the ground where its chances of releasing a seed that actually takes root are about one in 10,000. In fact, some cones will only open to drop their seed under the intense heat of a forest fire, thus ensuring a new generation after the devastation of the parent trees.

Flora

A complete selection of cone types found around Twin Peaks is available and reasonably priced at **Gilda's Card and Cheese Shop** on Route 21. While you're there, check out the cheese, too.

THIS WAY TO

STOP GHOSTWOOD

FASHION SHOW

Fauna

THE PINE WEASEL

The short-legged, furry Pine Weasel resembles the marten but is actually a member of the ferret family and closely related to the European polecat. Since references to it appear nowhere in Amerindian cultures, it is likely the creature was introduced to the New World by early settlers because of its excellent ability to ferret out rats. Hunted almost to extinction by growing boys and at the mercy of a shrinking habitat, this charming and harmless animal is the focus of our fight to stop Ghostwood Estates. As a symbol of our intrepid resolve, the Pine Weasel inspires each of us and is, all in all, just a real cute little bugger.

FAUNA

Northern Flying Squirrel - Unlike other squirrels, this creature is primarily nocturnal because it is one of the favorite foods for owls. Skin flaps on its sides between front and rear legs allow it to glide while its legs are used for balance and the tail as a rudder. Identified by their familiar "Whee" sound.

Striped Skunk - Found in forests and fields. All animals steer clear of these stinkers except one— very large owls.

Pine Weasel - Basically an arboreal animal, this is usually a nocturnal hunter, primarily for squirrels, though birds, insects and berries will do. Solitary animals, the males are extremely quarrelsome and have never been good at debate. 13 - 20 inches long, bushy tail and underparts are covered with dark fur, ecru on breast and throat; brown otherwise. Found primarily in pine forests. Endangered by the proposed **Ghostwood** development.

Beaver - 14" - 28". Once valued for its soft, water-resistant fur; presently the bane of the Army Corps of Engineers. Industrious but not very bright. Found near streams and ponds and in museums, stuffed.

Raccoon - Myth: they wash everything before eating it. Filthy garbage eaters in disguising masks.

Beaver Tracks

Grizzly Bear Claws

Brown Bear Claws

Black Bear Claws

Mule Deer - Avoids human areas more than white-tailed. Four to six feet in length. Males have antlers. Summer fur is reddish brown, winter fur gray. Browsers for feed. Can decimate new forests by over-browsing.

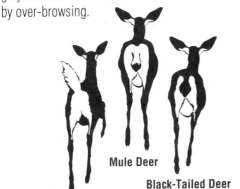

Mule Deer

Black-Tailed Deer

White-Tailed Deer

TAXIDERMY

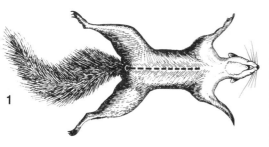

1

1 Slit the carcass from neck to anus. The skin around the abdomen and back should come away freely. Remove the feet at the ankle joints and pull the skin free of the rear legs.

2 Hang the carcass from a sturdy hook, and peel the skin downward. Cut carefully through the ear cartilidge, and around the eyes and mouth.

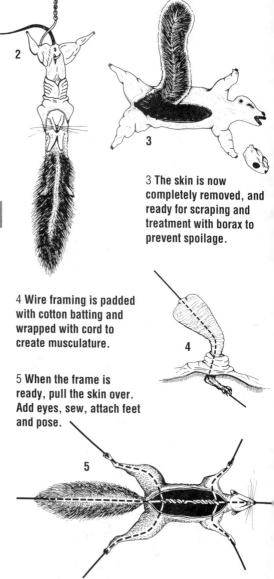

3 The skin is now completely removed, and ready for scraping and treatment with borax to prevent spoilage.

4 Wire framing is padded with cotton batting and wrapped with cord to create musculature.

5 When the frame is ready, pull the skin over. Add eyes, sew, attach feet and pose.

Fauna

Trim artificial ears to exact size, and mount on artificial skull *before* pulling skin over.

THE WHITE MOOSE

Out in present-day **Ghostwood National Forest**, beyond **Owl Cave**, is a craggy hillock from which rises an 85 foot tall **Ponderosa Pine**. Surrounded by marsh flats dotted with deer fern and lupines, it is a unique sight and one which has an important place in many **Snoqualmie** and **Cayuse** legends. It is here, beside the lone Ponderosa Pine, that the seldom-seen and sacred **White Moose** appears to those with troubled minds.

Early traders and explorers scoffed at Indian retellings of this singular beast emerging on moonlit nights as an imposing, iridescent ghost shimmering in the blue dark beside the Ponderosa, its head crowned with eight foot antlers and staring sadly over the meadow. Several diaries in the **County Museum** allude to the **White Moose** but only one diarist claimed to have seen it — **Dominick Renault**.

It is not easy to persuade a descendant of the **Snoqualmie** or **Cayuse** families to explain the origins of the **White Moose** legend or its significance in their cultures. One source, insisting her name be withheld, told us the **White Moose** appearing by the lone Ponderosa Pine was the sole survivor of a **Moose Massacre in 1787**; several dozen trappers herded more than 50 moose into the marsh flats and exterminated them, scalping the hides and antlers and leaving the remains for vultures and to rot. The lone **Ponderosa Pine** is the grave marker of those creatures. Drained of his brothers' and sisters' blood, the **White Moose** appears to those in trouble because it understands the agony of sorrow and despair.

Fauna

Moose tracks

So, if you are troubled in mind and spirit, make your way out past **Owl Cave** to the marsh flats and within sight of the lone **Ponderosa Pine** where, on a moonlit night, with only the sound of wind in the pine boughs behind you, you may be renewed by the melancholy and forgiving **White Moose**.

An Owl is never without a friend. Whatever an Owl's lot in life, wherever they may be, whether living or dead, they cannot be forgotten. For, at the mystical hour of eleven, the heart of Owldom enlarges

Fauna

and throbs with recollection. An Owl is forever, and in Twin Peaks the Owl Lodge on Sparkwood Road is always a haven for Brother Owls. 555-OWLS.

Owls Club—The elks that wander through our woods are a source of community pride. At one time, they roamed over most of the U.S. and Canada. Today their number has dwindled dangerously, especially west of the Rockies, where hunting has been indiscriminate. Elk are prized for their spectacular antlers. Peek into the entrance to the **Twin Peaks Owls Club**. The right-hand wall sports a rack that spans more than five feet. Or take a walk in the woods. You may be lucky enough to come upon one of these gentle giants munching on some **Douglas Fir** needles.

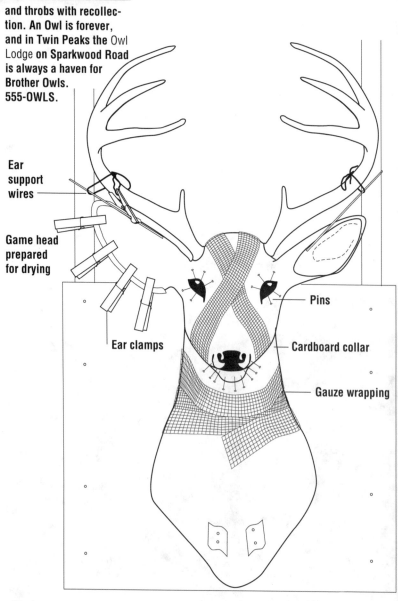

Ear support wires

Game head prepared for drying

Ear clamps

Pins

Cardboard collar

Gauze wrapping

ANTLERS

If you happen to take a late-fall walk through **Ghostwood National Forest** to view the foliage, you may be lucky enough to spot a **white-tail deer** sporting a full-grown set of antlers. There are few sights as magnificent. Elaborate and quite sharp, they rise out of the animal's head like a giant crown of thorns. If you've ever seen two deer in a head-to-head clash, you know how powerful a weapon antlers can be. If you've ever had the unforunate experience of going head to head with the head of an antlered deer in your car, you'll also know how devastating that can be. Highly recommended for repairs is **Headers By Hed**. [See ad, page 28.]

Deer are the only animals that grow antlers. Like horns, they are outgrowths of bone that are part of the animal's skull. Unlike horns, which are grown for life, often by both the male and female of such animals as cattle, sheep goats, and antelope, antlers are grown only by males, are shed every winter, and grow again in the early spring (in warmer climates they may be shed and regrow at other times of the year). New antlers are delicate and soft and grow rapidly. A thin layer of soft, fuzzy skin, called **velvet**, covers the budding antlers and helps to stimulate their growth. The velvet eventually dries up and is rubbed off by the deer. Full-grown, the antlers are hard, with a bony core, and extremely strong. Antlers differ widely in shape and size among the more than sixty species of deer. **Pete Martell** is responsible for the set of white-tail antlers hanging in the **Blue Pine Lodge**.

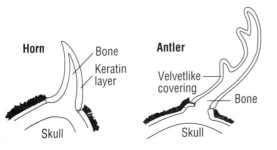

Horn
Bone
Keratin layer
Skull

Antler
Velvetlike covering
Bone
Skull

Great Horned Owl - 18" - 24", identified by widely-spaced ear tufts. Mottled brown back, light chest. Will attack any medium-sized mammal or bird. Gives off the familiar, muffled *hoot*. Male voice is higher-pitched than female; in concert they often harmonize in perfect thirds, though around Twin Peaks diminished sevenths are heard.

Faun

Yellow-Rumped Warbler - (Western species - Audubon's warbler). Yellow throat and crown and rump, otherwise black. A sassy, bright *chirp* call. Found in mixed forests. Good at parties.

Common Crow - 16 - 20" and all black. Most intelligent of birds; can count to three and four; possesses complex language and social structure, though extremely inept at commitment.

Turkey Vulture - 26" - 32" Wingspan: six feet. Nature's cleaner-upper; will eat virtually anything and is very beneficial to wilderness. Once very few, now proliferating and living virtually over entire U.S. and Canada.

CREATION OF THE OWL

A young man built a small hut for his mother-in-law beside his lodge. The old woman craved the intestines her daughter and husband ate rather than the beaver meat given to her. Luring her daughter into the woods to collect birch bark, the mother waited until the girl was in a tree before saying to her, "Daughter, say *Hu, Hu* and fly away." After initially refusing, the girl did as she was told, transformed into an owl and flew away, leaving her skin among the branches of the birch tree. The mother slipped into it.

That night the mother enjoyed the fat of beaver intestines before going to bed with her son-in-law. His wife landed atop the lodge. "Hu, Hu, you are sleeping with your mother-in-law." Already suspicious, the youth begged his wife to return. When she could not, he killed the mother-in-law and chased through the forest after his wife, imploring her to return. "I cannot," she said, "but you can say *Hu, Hu* and fly away with me." Repeating those words, he shed his skin and flew away with his wife as an owl.

THE EXTRAORDINARY
GREAT HORNED OWL

While most people know the eyesight of the Great Horned Owl allows it to see in virtual blackness (the lens enlarges and the eyeball actually alters in shape to bring the image-forming retina closer to the lens), few people are aware that the round facial disk giving this bird

Fauna

its other-worldly appear-ance is made up of short layers of stiff feathers around the edge of which is a trough that catches sounds too faint or high-pitched for the human ear. The sounds are funnelled to the ears behind the facial disk. Also, the ears are not symmetrical; sounds will arrive at one ear before the other, allowing the bird to triangulate the source of the sound. If you're quiet and very patient, and can find your way in the dark, spend the night in Ghostwood National Forest and you may spy one of these miraculous creatures.

OWLWISE BY FIRELIGHT

The flames sway on the logs. Firelight dances with shadows on the forest wall around us while the stars have formed a rippling blanket overhead. A cub of burning birch hisses. It pops and showers the perimeter with sparks. Beyond, the darkness is filled with unseen movement. Out of the Neolithic past, the *hu-hu*'s of a **Great Horned Owl** are joined by the *hu* of their mate to form a perfect third. Not dread but a connection with our past is what we feel, a thread running back to the artless creatures we once were when we first heard those oboe-like notes from the **Great Horned Owl**. In Paleolithic times, we suspected omens in its voice, heard in it questions we were unable to articulate but which have stayed within us, incomplete and taunting. We are certain that ancient, taloned bird sees what we do not, knows what we never will. And some night, silent as a gliding feather, its immensity will engulf us at fireside to tell us things we want to know as well as those we don't. In the shadowed forest we're pulled by that lurking and alluring ghost and we are enthralled.

Fauna

47

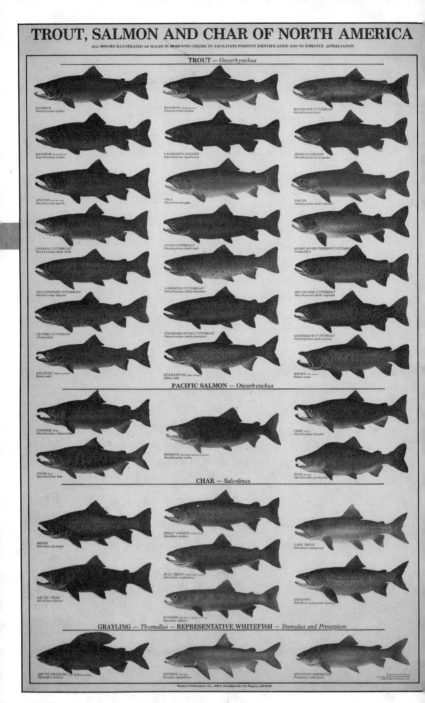

TROUT, SALMON AND CHAR OF NORTH AMERICA

ALL SPECIES ILLUSTRATED AS MALES IN SPAWNING COLORS TO FACILITATE POSITIVE IDENTIFICATION AND TO ENHANCE APPRECIATION

For information on how to order the poster above, see page 112.

PETE MARTELL: LANDING THAT BIG ONE

I've been fishing the streams and lakes around Twin Peaks since my dad first introduced me to it when I was five. A lot of that first day went by like a dream, I suspect, so I can't remember exactly what he said when I knocked his tacklebox into the rapids or when my line got twisted around him and he slipped into the stream, but he had a rich vocabulary and I sure bet he let out with a couple of hundred dollar expressions.

The streams flowing out of and in to **Black** and **Pearl** lakes support a variety of fish. There are river types such as salmon and trout (and, for the record, **Ben Horne** may claim he caught that 45 inch sockeye on display at the **Great Northern Hotel** but he didn't; I did) and there are stillwater fish such as pike, bass, bluegill and perch. My favorite are sockeye and cutthroat because they're crafty devils and fierce fighters and they taste just superb fried up in a little oil and butter.

Over the years I've developed some pretty canny, sure-fire methods for hooking that Big One. Here they are:

A Know what's hatching and what the fish are 'rising' to. If you're new to an area or an inexperienced angler, find the local bait and tackle shop. Here in Twin Peaks, **Mort Zafkee** owns the **Fish or Cut Bait Shop** and can tell you what flies will bring in that "Big One". But don't think you can tie on a Muddler when the steelheads are rising to a Green Butt Skunk.

B Be aware of your equipment's strengths and limitations. Only a fool would take a 7 1/2 ft., 3 1/2 oz. rod to go after Sockeye; you'd snap off the tip trying to place the fly. Likewise, you wouldn't tie a 4/0 1/2 hook angling for perch; it just tears the heck out of their mouths when you try to pull it out and that's if they can get their mouths around it.

C Don't talk to the fish. For one thing, it distracts them from hunting and feeding and, for another, they won't understand you anyway.

PETE MARTELL—**Born June 28, 1934, Pete demonstrated at a remarkably early age an affinity for moving small objects. After the family's cutlery was retrieved from various rooms in the house, Pete was given a chessboard and the rest is history. Pete is also the most uxorious man in Twin Peaks and can tie a Duncan Loop in the dark.**

BESTS: The pentannual Passion Play; a steelhead rising to a Green Butt Skunk.

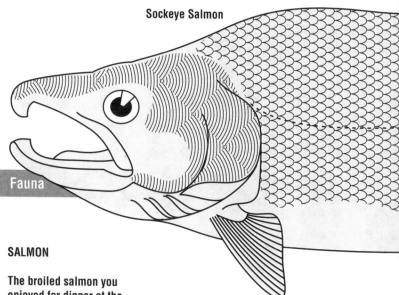

Sockeye Salmon

Fauna

SALMON

The broiled salmon you enjoyed for dinner at the Lamplighter Inn **was no doubt a Chinook salmon, named after the** Chinook Indians, **legendary fishermen whose religion concentrated on the first salmon rite, a ritual enacted to welcome the annual salmon run. The Chinook's entire economy was based on salmon; dried fish were often traded among the neighboring tribes for various goods. As fishermen in Twin Peaks do today, the Chinook fished the abundant waters of the Columbia River, which eventually feeds into the Pacific Ocean.**

It's possible to observe the annual run if you come here in early autumn. The Twin Peaks Chamber of Commerce **sponsors early morning trips to the river, where, if**

D Check the weather forecast. This sounds simple, but if you're doing stream fishing it doesn't hurt to know what's happening at the headwaters. Flooding can be quick and take you by surprise. For lake fishing, remember this jingle:

> *Red sky at morning, anglers take warning*
> *Red sky at night, anglers delight.*

I think that's it, anyway.

E Be sure you're properly equipped. I just dumped out my tacklebox to inventory what's in it. Pretty interesting, though it made an awful mess on the rug.

Continued margin page 51

50

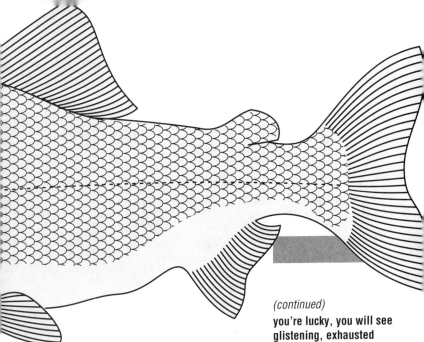

1 Two dozen dry flies speared onto a slab of foam rubber

2 Spools of 5 and 10 lb. test line

3 2 1/2, 4 1/2 and 6 lb test leader (tippet)

4 Several swivel snaps (lake fishing)

5 Scissors for cutting line and trimming knots

6 Pliers for removing hooks from fish and the nape of your neck.

7 Swiss Army Knife (indispensable)

8 Churchkey (indispensable)

9 Fishing license (don't leave home without one)

10 Sunglasses, not broken like mine

11 Spare reel

12 Some paper clips

13 Half a dozen nails

14 Shot glass

15 Several books of useless matches

16 Some shirt buttons

17 Chess board (6"x6")

18 Rabbit's foot I thought I lost

19 Train ticket to Spokane

20 Kiwanis medal

21 Recipe for Osso Bucco

(continued)

you're lucky, you will see glistening, exhausted salmon who have for months been swimming upstream from the ocean, fearlessly battling all sorts of obstacles, from rapid currents to water-falls. Salmon always return for spawning to the same stream in which they hatched. It seems they have an extraordi-nary ability to navigate by sensing the earth's magnetic field and the ocean's currents. Once they reach the coast, they pick up the scent of their birth stream and follow it home.

A magnificent (45 inches from nose to tail!) salmon is on display in the main office of the Great Northern. **Both** Pete Martell **and** Ben Horne claim they caught it — you decide. If you're lucky enough to hook a big one yourself, the folks at Tim and Tom's Taxi and Taxidermy **can prepare it for your wall at home.**

Fauna

Some items may appear unnecessary to the novice's eye but that's the thing about angling; you never know, so be prepared.

F Know what sort of fish you're likely to catch. It never ceases to amaze me the way folks go after trout with a Western Green Drake in a wide stream of some depth where it's more likely salmon are feeding. Likewise, don't expect salmon in riffle water.

G If a brown bear wants that salmon on the end of your line, let him or her have it.

H And, finally, know how many fish you are legally allowed to have in your possession. Any extra, hide them in case a game warden comes nosing around.

HAPPY ANGLING!

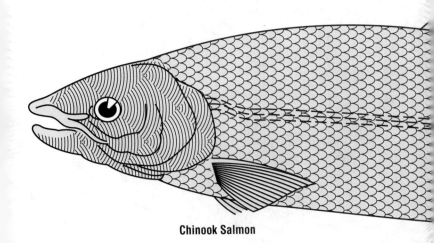

Chinook Salmon

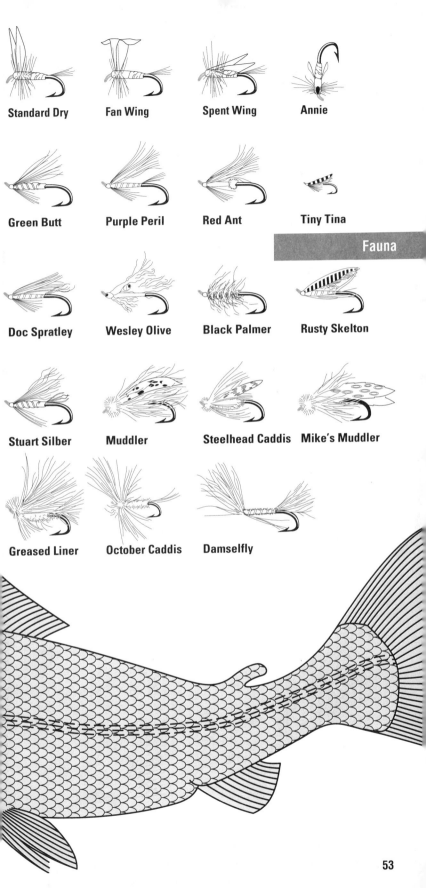

Standard Dry

Fan Wing

Spent Wing

Annie

Green Butt

Purple Peril

Red Ant

Tiny Tina

Doc Spratley

Wesley Olive

Black Palmer

Rusty Skelton

Stuart Silber

Muddler

Steelhead Caddis

Mike's Muddler

Greased Liner

October Caddis

Damselfly

ED HURLEY—**Born October 26, 1950.** A most unlikely Scorpio and unaware of it, Big Ed is convinced his birthday is

October 26 and he's right. He also is right about anything having to do with American-built engines though the vagaries of human nature generally baffle and elude him. A graduate of Twin Peaks High, he enjoys a good cup of coffee and an intimate conversation at the Double R Diner.

BESTS: Beaver Fritters, the Passion Play, the odor of crankcase oil, the Packard Timber Games.

Big Ed's Gas Farm—this used to be the beach.

TWIN PEAKS: IN THE BEGINNING

It is astonishing, but perhaps appropriate that the present site of Twin Peaks was, a billion or so years ago, the western edge—the coast—of North America and where **Big Ed's Gas Farm** now stands was then a coastal plain and beach, though it is unlikely sunbathing was allowed.

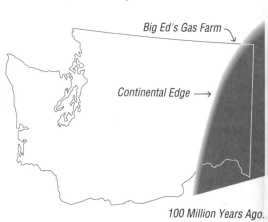

Big Ed's Gas Farm

Continental Edge →

100 Million Years Ago.

Around 200 million years ago, the Macro continent called 'Pangaea' split up; North and South America moved away from Europe. The then west coast began moving further west, shoving the Pacific floor beneath it and creating from the collision granitic magma, some of which erupted in volcanic formation. Thus, most rock around Twin Peaks is metamorphic **granite**, **gneiss** and **schist**, some of it more than two billion years old.

One hundred million years later, a large island about the size of California (but not as self-absorbed) called the Okanagan subcontinent slammed into North America and crushed the continental shelf back, creating **volcanic activity** (likely elevating **White Tail** and **Blue Pine Mountains**) and forming the buckled layers of sedimentary rock to the west of present day Twin Peaks known as the Kootenay Arc.

The next great geological alteration began some two to three million years ago and continued throughout Pleistocene times—**glaciation**. Geologists are not certain what destabilized the earth's climate to bring on the Ice Ages but it is certain that northern Washington was covered by sheets of ice as thick as a mile between one and .5 million years ago. As these massive glaciers melted, immense basins were formed. Once undammed, they plunged through sedimentary and granite layers, creating the spectacular gorges and valleys around Twin Peaks, most dramatically seen at **White Tail Falls** and east of the town around the **Pearl Lakes**.

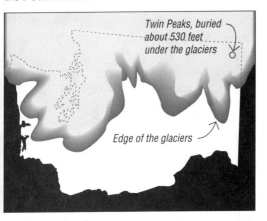

Twin Peaks, buried about 530 feet under the glaciers

Edge of the glaciers

All three rock types are well-represented around Twin Peaks: **sedimentary**, formed from the ocean floor before it was pushed up out of the sea (shell fossils are found in high elevations of the mountains); **igneous**, melted by subsequent volcanic action; **metamorphic**, created by extreme heat and pressure.

Geologists consider the area around Twin Peaks remarkably youthful, displaying geologic experiments in progress: earthquakes and faulting continue; glaciation occurring in the high mountains; volcanoes resting in expectation of future eruptions.

1224.5 in

984 in

g Weather

74.5 in

Big Ed

WEATHER WATCH

In planning your visit and experience in Twin Peaks, you should know that, according to the **Twin Peaks Gazette**, our average July temperature is 66 degrees Fahrenheit; January temperature is 30 degrees Fahrenheit; and the average yearly precipitation is 38 inches. We get lots of **frost.**

Our local meteorological expert and all-around savant, **Roice Foley**, tells us the greatest snow fall in all North America in one season was 1224.5 inches at Washington's **Rainer Paradise Ranger Station** from February 1971 to February 1972. That same year, Twin Peaks had a snowfall of 984 inches, which dropped 74.5 inches on the town in the first five hours when it abruptly stopped for a day.

When hiking and biking and otherwise enjoying nature around **Twin Peaks**, be aware that weather changes can be sudden, unexpected, contrary and plain vicious. **Be prepared.** And remember: The mountains don't care; we do.

THE BLIZZARD OF 1889

There are as many versions of the **Great Blizzard of 1889** as there were survivors. Two words, however, appear in every recollection of the cataclysm: *ferocious* and *unexpected*.

Our first report that something unusual was about to occur comes from **Reverend Isaiah Hurly**'s memoirs: "Dec. 19th. Clear. Endeavoring to see ailing **Bartholomew Beaufort** up by the base of **Blue Pine** [mountain], I could not control my horse; she shied adamantly and I was forced to turn back. Unexpected cold surprised me, too."

So apparently complacent was the town that the **Annual Candlelighting and Christmas Tree Ceremony** on **Meadowlark Hill** enters expectantly into many diary entries of that day. "It is only 3PM," wrote **Millicent Revere**, "and dozens of families are romping the streets, spreading seasonal joy and affixing candles to the boughs of pine trees on the hill."

What caught everyone in Twin Peaks by surprise was a meteorological anomaly: the storm approached from the Northeast out of Alberta and Southeast British Columbia Provinces. Accustomed to weather patterns from the northwest, all eyes saw only clear skies above **White Tail Mountain.**

From diaries and newspapers we can conclude with some certainty that more than 2,000 people had assembled for the Christmas ceremony. From her bedroom window overlooking the festivities, feverish and 'feeling poorly' **Cynthia Sithe** saw, "a gathering of celebrating, happy people about the hill, while beyond them a ferocious gathering of ominous black clouds piling atop each other as though racing for some undetermined but pernicious goal and encouraged by a devilish, malignant fury."

A horrible note was struck by **Knut Zimmerman** when he wrote, "I stood beside **Pete Lindstrom** when that ferocious and unexpected wind hit the town like a malevolent fist and drove a candle from one of the fir boughs into the back of his head where it actually quivered and hummed for a moment before Pete dropped down dead."

More than forty-three citizens perished within the first ten minutes of the blizzard. Another three dozen were likely blinded by the awful and awesome white snow and lost their way.

A telling entry is found in **Katy Mullen**'s diary, James Packard's Secretary wrote on December 21st, "Coffins are stacked head-high in the **Opera House**. I will never see a play or concert there again, it is so horrible. I was told some bodies were too frozen in grotesque ways to be fitted into their mortal boxes and limbs had to literally be sawed off from their torsos. **Mr. Packard** is glum and his mood ferocious & dark. It is unusual for him to be so. I heard him mutter to the stuffed and mounted **Great Horned Owl** in his office, 'What have we done, this town, our people, that you cannot warn us of such calamity? We are industrious. Why are we not blessed?'

This obituary appeared in the *Twin Peaks Gazette*:

Ge — Weather

IN
MEMORIAM

Elsie Spaeth Miller

Beloved wife and mother, mourned by her husband and son and daughter. Killed cruelly by the ferocious blizzard and no reason why.

We love and will miss her.

Sic transit Gloria Mundi.

Tim & Tom's Taxidermy

Through the magic of telepathy, blind Tom pictures vividly everything his brother says. Born in Twin Peaks, never having left for anything, the brothers are inseparable. The only time they're not working is when they're sleeping - and even then they're sawing logs.

Tom says: "Don't be nervous, just close your eyes like me."

Come ride and stuff with us.

Tim says: "Tom's blind...come ride in back with me I'll drive."

WHITE TAIL FALLS

More than 350,000 visitors travel to Twin Peaks every year, to fish, hike, attend the county fair (and to help judge the annual cherry and huckleberry pie contests!), go bird watching, river rafting, log rolling, and to gape at our glorious White Tail Falls, which are even taller (though not as wide) than the Niagra Falls.

Two hundred forty-eight million gallons plummet six hundred feet down the falls every hour, generat-

ng a lot of electrical energy and an awesome rainbow on sunny days. The **Packard Mill**, which was situated next to the falls, originally drew its power from the torrent. Today, it is the raw power of this force of nature, the sheer drama of its beauty, that holds anyone fortunate enough to stand near by, in its spell.

The **Twin Peaks Chamber of Commerce** sponsors bus trips to the falls every afternoon at 3:00PM rain or shine, meet in front of Town Hall. Just one piece of advice: wear a raincoat, rubber boots, and bring your umbrella!

MEET YOUR LOVE

So magical are the powers of White Tail Falls **that anyone who has ever fallen in love within the sound of their plunging water remains in love forever.**

OWL CAVE

It is through the local Indians that we first learned of **Owl Cave**. It they did not carve the cave out of the landscape, they certainly discovered it. The **Flathead Tribe** used the cave to store pelts, hold meetings and elude their enemies. They also instilled the cave with great power and legend, saying that the cave was visited by the "Beyond" and that there had been "messages left" for them there. But, curiously, for a cave bearing such lofty legend, not much has been found of the time—no artifacts, drawings or the like.

The first white men to stumble onto, or into as it were, the cave were two confused Spanish trappers, **Edwardo Delegato** and former prison inmate **José "Shorteyes" Manuela**, who huddled in the cave during the **blizzard of 1889**. As the blizzard howled outside, legend tells us, they built a small but comfortable blaze and made shadowy images on the wall with their hands that resemble the court of **Queen Isabella**.

Recently found.

Brochures of the time tell us that through the 1920's the cave was a popular spot to "take your favorite flapper and your second hand ukelele" and strum tunes of eternal love. As a newspaper report from the time tells, "There were enough hopes and dreams discussed in that cave to make Ali Baba green with envy."

Owl Cave played a great part in the apprehension of the **Phelan Gang** that robbed a bank in Twin Peaks in the spring of 1933. They eluded an all-out search for the greater part of a day, but upon nightfall soon surrendered when the head of the gang, the bloodthirsty **Milo Phelan**, became frightened by the dark and built a fire.

President Truman visited the cave in 1948 on the campaign trail and became an honorary member of the **Flathead Tribe**. Soon after, the

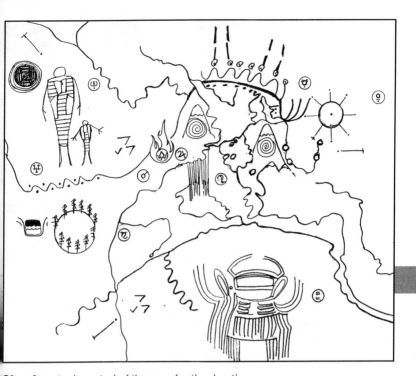

Circulars took control of the cave for the duration of Truman's presidency. During that time it was referred to as "**Elk Cave**," a moniker that was never taken seriously by anyone in the community.

Of late, the cave has held little interest for the town, except for the general opinion that it is a "darn good spot for a six pack and a sandwich." As **Mayor Milford** has said, "Radio killed the cave for me." Where once there were grand celebrations on the day of the capture of the **Phelan Gang** or on the anniversary of the blizzard, it now is mostly visited by couples who decided to get married here, or by those seeking to do a little reminiscing about the good ol' days, or by older members of the **Flathead Tribe** for religious reasons.

Still, when visiting the town, **Owl Cave** is a place to go and see and confront its grand history. A place to sit and virtually close your eyes and think about stuff.

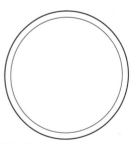

Circulars

The Circular Lodge **is a secret society of brothers and all interested parties are respectfully asked, with love and affection, to take their questions elsewhere. We will continue to do good deeds in our own characteristically mysterious ways. On Highway J. 555-6969.**

THE GRANGE

Arguably the grandest edifice ever built in Twin Peaks, and a marvel of architecture, was **The Grange**, built in 1904. The only building to remain undamaged in the **Smallish Earthquake of 1905**, it housed the Sheriff's Office, County Seat, Chamber of Commerce, Voting Hall, Patrons of Husbandry and Pierre's Smoke and News Arcade.

Two giant 22'6" stories in height, **The Grange** was built of **Douglas Fir**, milled and sized by the **Packard Mill**. All who visited this remarkable building accounted it a wonder and its architect, **Winston Sanford White**, received numerous kudos [*see*: Mailer, N. *Redemption in Wood and Marble: The Twin Peaks Grange*. Architrave Press: Tacoma, 1949).

The business life of early Twin Peaks revolved around this building which stood to the north between the present-day Highway J and the old railroad spur. Also the hub of politics, it was the scene of several bloody riots during the **Timber Wars** of 1906-7. As more and more workers poured into the area for employment at the two competing mills, spirits ran high, fanned by Unionists and Anarchists, and meetings at the **Grange** erupted in fist fights. **James Packard**'s famous speech of 1908 [*see*: Johnson, A.P. *Some Pretty Good Speeches I Have Heard*. Vanity Press: Ashtabula, 1913) ended with these spell-binding words:

Mankind shall not wallow and drown in the pockets of anarchy. O tannenbaum, O tannenbaum fear this rising horde for they will ravish you and pay only in wooden nickels!

Indeed, much of Twin Peaks' history swirled around the old, graceful building. Presidential nominee **Harry S. Truman** spoke on the steps of the **Grange** in 1948.

Half a decade later, however, the building's political life was ashes. During a snowstorm on December

TRUMAN

In 1948 on a campaign tour of the western United States, future President Harry S. Truman **spoke sage and witty words on the steps of Twin Peaks'** Grange **building. As he was stepping onto his train after the speech, the soon-to-be-President accepted the hand of** Boyd Truman, **millworker and father of present day Twin Peaks'** Sheriff Harry S. Truman. **No one knows if** Boyd **asked permission but everyone knows where** Sheriff Truman**'s Christian name came from.**

1, 1953, it burst into flame. Before the blackened marble cracked in the heat and the glowing-red beams buckled, horrified onlookers heard the building let out a rasping sigh. In an instant it crumbled into a mountain of smoking debris. Once arson was established as the cause, suspicion and paranoia gripped the community. The witch hunt that ensued pitted neighbor against neighbor. The case has never been officially closed, and to this day, no one has been charged with the crime.

THE TRAIN GRAVEYARD

At the end of the old Railroad Spur across the Washington-Idaho border is a silent community of once magnificent creatures that brought to this land an era of unparalleled wealth and excitement. They were kings in this wilderness. Now the land has reclaimed them; their life's blood seeps into the rich soil in streams the color of rust.

For decades the great trains carried lumber from Twin Peaks to the world. In the 1950s, however, lumber transport by truck became more economical as the United States highway system linked rural America to its major cities. The Great Railroad Era was over.

These behemoths of industry, the dynamic giants of locomotion, lie side by side—cars of the **Union Pacific** adjacent to **James J. Hill's Great Northern** locomotives. They are silent. But could they express themselves, they would no doubt sing in deep-throated chords describing their awe-somely muscular past. Now, together in their graveyard, they witness things which, could they tell us, would chill our bones and rob our nights of sleep.

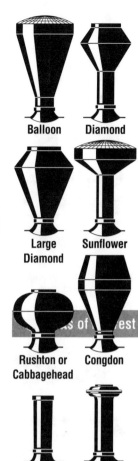

Balloon
Diamond
Large Diamond
Sunflower
Rushton or Cabbagehead
Congdon
Straight Cannon
Capstack

Twelve **Douglas Firs** describe a circle. They appear strong enough to support the sky and their collective age stretches back almost to the Pleistocene. You want the giants to speak, tell you of the amazing history running along their grain in which the never ending Quest is given substance. You feel close to the Beginning.

It is **Glastonberry Grove** you're standing in, a part of **Ghostwood National Forest** and backdrop for Twin Peaks' pentannual **Passion Play**. (Every five years or so).

The Passion Play is one of the mysteries of Twin Peaks.

Of uncertain date and origin, the **Passion Play** continues to evolve and is a profoundly moving ceremony. While a precise day and time are never announced, if you're in town during the month of April and keep your eyes and ears open you can follow the quiet exodus of the curious and converted out to **Glastonberry Grove** shortly after dark to gather around the twelve **Great Firs**. From the shadows, half a dozen cassocked figures emerge bearing sword, chrysanthemum, crucifix and chalice. There appears the mysterious guardian at the gate. To this day no one knows where the guardian comes from or why it appears. Mystery also surrounds the sponsors of the event but rumors suggest the ultra-secret **Bookhouse Boys**.

Armpatch of the Bookhouse Boys. This ultra-secret group of guys seems to sponsor the Passion Play

Lasting the entire night, dawn brings the ceremony's climax when sunlight obliterates darkness as Good vanquishes Evil. Skeptics may wonder what happens if the day dawns cloudy. In fact, in the entire recorded history of the ceremony that has never occurred; dawn of Twin Peaks' **Passion Play** has always been announced by sunlight.

The next **Passion Play** will occur sometime in April, 1992. No need to call, just be there.

PACKARD TIMBER GAMES

In August, citizens and visitors flock to Sparkwood Road, 1/2 a mile north of the Route 21 traffic light, for the annual **Packard Timber Games**. Established in 1910 by **James Packard** as a means of promoting ideals of sportsmanship and manliness among his employees, the games combine events from the Ancient Highland Games of Scotland and competitions created by the **Packard Mill** loggers over the decades since the mill's founding.

The seven events are:

1 Caber Toss - A 16 foot fir trunk weighing 80 to 100 lbs. is tossed by flipping it upward so that the lead end strikes the ground and the other end falls forward, *not* backward. Distance tossed is not a factor, only accuracy, and a pole that ends up lying at 12 o'clock from the point where it was tossed is most 'accurate.'

2 Spinoff - On a floating pine trunk in **Black Lake**, two contestants square off. Wearing caulked boots and wielding cant sticks, they spin the log and the winner of the event is the one who remains on the log while the losers struggle to keep from being sucked over **Black Lake Dam**.

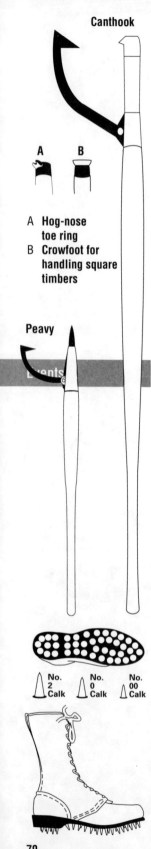

Canthook

A   **B**

A **Hog-nose toe ring**
B **Crowfoot for handling square timbers**

Peavy

Events

No.
2
Calk

No.
0
Calk

No.
00
Calk

3 Sheaf Pitch - A 15 lb. bundle of spruce or pine boughs is tossed over a horizontal bar with a pitchfork. After each successful toss the bar is raised 2". In 1938, **Bernie Welch** tossed a sheaf more than 30' into the air. Unfortunately, the pitchfork went with the boughs, came free in mid-air and pinned a spectator's beret to his head.

4 High Climb - Using climbing irons and caulked boots as well as a 'life belt,' a 40' tall trunk is scaled. The contestant doing so in the least amount of time wins. Falling immediately disqualifies a competitor unless they can prove they were pushed.

5 Bury the Hatchet - Actually, it's a double-edged Western Falling Axe that contestant's toss at a stationary wooden target using only one hand. Sometimes called 'the one-armed bandit,' distance and accuracy are both factors here. With each successful throw the contestant steps back two feet. **Deputy Hawk** consistently wins this most demanding event.

6 Stone Throw - Any idiot can figure out what this event requires except that, unlike the Olympic Shotput and Hammer Toss, no wind-up is allowed. This means most of the 22 lb. stones aren't thrown very far and just sort of plop dully onto the ground.

7 Trunk Chop - Standing atop a horizontal trunk from 6 to 8 feet in diameter, contestants wield an old-style Western Falling Axe. **Sean Ladoux**, in 1955, set a record of chopping through a 6 1/2 foot trunk in 37 minutes, though it took him less than a second to chop off his right toe while winning the event. **Sean** had it bronzed and bequeathed to Twin Peaks' **County Museum** whose curator misplaced it sometime in the mid 1980's.

Dress: All entrants, male and female, must wear kilts. Plaid or solid is optional.

THE PROPERLY HUNG AXE

Other than keeping a keen edge, hanging an axe is the most critical adjustment you can make and should not be rushed.

1 Firmly grasp the stock (handle and stock are the same thing) in one hand.

2 With the other hand, bring the head into line with the stock, keeping the eyehole of the head directly in line with the butt and in the 'open' position.

Events

3 Gently insert the stock into the aperture, being sure not to bruise the wood and keeping in mind that the 'fit' should be very tight and may require considerable pressure.

4 Do not hammer the head onto the stock. If the 'fit' is too tight, tap the bottom of the stock on a hard surface and allow the weight of the head to impale itself onto the stock.

5 Once the head is properly 'seated,' a wedge or shim of hardwood or metal may have to be driven into the stock to set and properly 'hang' the head.

6 Your axe should now be properly hung.

Twin Peaks is a beehive of communal activity. We love our town to pieces and welcome all visitors to join in at any time. Our calendar may not be full, but each event is choice. Give our **Twin Peaks Chamber of Commerce** a call to confirm dates: 555-TPCC.

DECEMBER

If Thanksgiving was a bust or you blew out on too much turkey, there's no need to worry; flagging spirits always revive on the second Saturday in December when we celebrate the coming holidays in our annual **Candlelighting and Christmas Tree Ceremony**. Gather, if you will, at 10AM on **Meadowlark Hill** for the preschoolers' **Magi Pageant** with real camels and sheep. All day long the air is filled with seasonal tunes as carolers stroll through town in turn-of-the-century costumes trying to out-sing each other. The novelty is good for about half an hour, but we're a tolerant community. Shortly after dusk, everyone gathers in front of **Horne's Department Store** where the current **Miss Twin Peaks** throws the switch that lights all the firs and pines downtown (after first observing a moment of silence in memory of Miss Twin Peaks '73 who was electrocuted during the ceremony that year). Then it's ice skating at the town rink until the owls come out.

JANUARY

After the **New Year** we like to leave time for tempers to cool down and gifts to be returned or exchanged for cash. But come the third weekend of January, the fabulous Scandinavian tradition of **Winterskol** sounds off with the "Reindeer Vaterstag Anthem" played on Alpenhorns from the roof of the **Great Northern Hotel** at 7AM Saturday morning. Throughout the festive day Glugg flows liberally as we demonstrate just about everything you can do with snow and ice and some things you shouldn't. The **Ice Castle Competition** is in front of the high school, the **Skaters'**

Events

Jamboree at the municipal rink and the **Lion's Club Snow and Slush Breakfast** from 9 to noon in the Timber Room. Saturday night the **Boy Scouts** cross country ski (or rollerblade if there's no snow) through town by candlelight. Those not stupid with Glugg by nightfall gather for the **Big Dance** at the high school.

FEBRUARY

Two weeks into February, chess players are boning up on their Sicilian Defense and Snoqualmie Stalemate in preparation for our annual **Chess Tournament** at the **Great Northern Hotel**. Begun by **Andrew Packard** in 1953 and currently presided over by soon-to-be-Grandmaster **Pete Martell,** the tournament is open to all. Former challengers include **Vladimir Nabokov**, among others. **Anatoly Karpov** once sent his regrets but the framed letter has disappeared from its display in the Icelandic Room. The tournament boasts as its grand prize a free weekend for three at the **Great Northern Hotel** and some books.

MARCH

On March 17th Twin Peakers wake up expectantly in anticipation of that day's **Caribou Festival**. Held in place of the somewhat dubious **St. Patrick's Day**, this is nevertheless a robust and spirited event to which people from many miles around flock, all dressed from head to toe in the fur of dead animals. Roaming the town shortly after the bars open, bands of roisterers compete for the most accurate imitation of the caribou mating call. The contest is unofficial; the winner usually determined by a fist fight. Beer and ale flow, jokes are ribald and **Sheriff Truman** cancels all leave for his deputies.

APRIL

The Yellow Lupine Festival is one of April's highlights. Usually awash in color as spring and cabin fever have ceased to devastate the citizenry, Twin Peaks holds a 10K run for the fit, a parade with marching bands and floats and then crowns **Miss Twin Peaks.** This popular event gives the young women of our town an opportunity to demonstrate charm, poise, intelligence and talent. Virtually every girl between sixteen and eighteen tries out for the honor and is judged on qualities important to our community by former Miss Twin Peaks **Norma Jennings** and **Richard Tremayne** and **Mayor Milford**. Following the **Coronation Ceremony** is the **Light Up My Life Ball** at the Country Club. Most everyone is welcome.

MAY

Spring is really upon us when the **PEO**, a secret women's philanthropic society, sponsors the **Gardens and Homes Tour**. Bursting with color and fertility, the gardens are merely used as an excuse to get some idea what goes on behind closed doors in other people's homes. Of course, they've all been cleaned and scrubbed so neurotically the owners often have difficulty recognizing their own furniture. Contact the PEO for exact dates and times; 555-1414, though there's seldom anyone there.

Events

JULY

School's been out for awhile, the heat has not quite set in and Twin Peaks is up for a party! **The Fourth of July Celebration** is our big summer event. It begins with the **Innertube Race** down the river below **White Tail Falls**, after which someone is usually killed trying to go over the Falls in a barrel. Over in the park you'll be delighted by the **Herring Relay Race**, the **Sack Race** and the **Frog Jumping Contest**, won consecutively for the last ten years by Toad of Double R Diner fame. Meanwhile, Antique cars are circling the park and the **Great Northern Hotel** hosts the **Doughnut Walk**, sponsored by **Wagon Wheel Bakery**. Most popular, of course, is the **Pie-eating Contest** that takes place in the parking lot of the **Double R Diner**. At night the Owls Club pyrotechnics wizard, **Angelo Wong**, proves that the Italians know just as much about fireworks as the Chinese by shooting off a half hours' worth accompanied by our High School Band playing the "1812 Overture" by Felix Mendelssohn.

AUGUST

In August, pack your picnic basket (or let Norma Jennings at the **Double R** do it for you) and come out for theatre between the bleachers at the **Senior High School** where the **Twin Peaks Timber Players** will be on the stage once again [see page 106]. They never fail to transport us to other climes and show us passions we only dream of. This talented band of amateur thespians will enthrall you with the breadth of their feeling, and their hilarious comedic timing, (especially their leading character actress who always receives a standing ovation— and I don't mind admitting I do).

SEPTEMBER

Bringing the summer to a close and kicking in the fall is perhaps the biggest, best attended event of the year. Nothing gets this town more excited than the **Packard Timber Games** [see page 69]. Held over Labor Day Weekend, these events allow the men of our town to demonstrate their virility and equipoise in seven strenuously demanding events. Everybody picnics on the sidelines because they can't take their eyes off the sweating, muscled and kilted contestants vying to take home the **Wooden Thing**. The potential for humiliation is intense, so there's always a pretty big crowd of laughers and jeerers to belittle the wimps and losers. It's spine-tingling fun and something to tell your grandchildren about.

Events

OCTOBER

After the trees have lost their leaves, when the aroma of burning wood spreads out from smoking chimneys, everyone knows that just around the corner is the **Twin Peaks Halloween Parade**, sponsored by the **Twin Peaks Chamber of Commerce** and **Horne's Department Store**. The parade route between the high school and the Senior high school on Meadowlark Hill is lined with jack-o-lanterns, each lit by a burning candle. The high school float is first and it depicts an event from our fascinating history such as the **Smallish Earthquake of 1905** or the Grange Fire. Following this are dozens of children in homemade costumes bearing sparklers like a parade of fireflies. Then the **Horne** float appears. In past years **Amory Battis** stood atop the float costumed like a Druid and everyone always wondered why. Mr. Battis' recent death is a great loss to some, but especially to the parade.

In Twin Peaks, though, Halloween isn't just for kids. The adults come dressed up as Greek Satyrs and peg-legged Pirates. **Ogres, serial killers** and **wicked witches** are also very popular and it's a treat to hear the preschoolers wailing in terror at the effect of the adults' vivid costumes and convincing portrayals; everyone gets a good-natured laugh to see the toddlers so terrified. Finally, the parade wags its tail to the high school where the late **Dougie Milford**, founder and publisher of the *Twin Peaks Gazette* and brother of Dwayne the mayor, used to muse on the restorative powers of terror and darkness. Then everyone repairs to the cafeteria for doughnuts, grape Kool-Aid and hot chocolate. Also available is coffee.

LUMBERJACK FEAST

People say the **Sunday Lumberjack Breakfast** held at the **Twin Peaks Fire Department** is the country's most calorific spread. A tradition in Twin Peaks, the monthly feast features three kinds of pancakes, two kinds of waffles, eggs prepared in every possible way, homebaked muffins, fresh fruit and vegetable concentrates, link and pattie sausages, scrapple, home and French fried potatoes, beaver fritters, jams, marmalades, and a full bar. It lasts from 6:30AM until 3AM Held on the last Sunday of the month, you can enter the pancake-eating contest. So far, no one has topped **Ed Hurley**'s record—last March he ate 110 pancakes in twenty minutes, and lived to tell about it!

Everything is delicious, and, of course, the coffee is legendary. Held rain, shine, or snow. Call 911 for more information.

CHERRY PIE RECIPE

Ingredients: 3 cups cherries fresh frozen
1 cup bakers sugar
1/8 tsp salt
1 cup water
4 Tbs. cornstarch w-13

Directions:

3 cups cherries

Thaw cherries overnight at room temperature.

2 cups juice
1 cup water
(add more or less water to yield 3 cups)

Drain cherries through a colander. This should yield 2 cups juice. Add 1 cup of water making a total of 3 cups juice. Reserve 1 cup juice for cornstarch mix.

1 cup juice cooled
4 Tbs w-13 cornstarch

Dissolve cornstarch in cooled liquid, stir with whip.

2 cups juice
2/3 cup bakers sugar
1/8 tsp salt

Bring juice, sugar and salt to a boil. At boiling point
add cornstarch mix (step 3) and cook until clear,
about 5 minutes. **If cooked too long syrup
gets gummy.**

1/3 cup bakers sugar

Take step 4 off fire and stir in sugar. Blend thoroughly.

Completed cooked juice

Pour completed cooked juice over drained cherries
(step 1) and blend with spoon. Cool. **IMPORTANT**:
Stir completed mix while cooling to prevent scum
from forming on top.

Pour in 8" pie crust shell. Top completed pie with
lattice crust. Bake at 425 degrees for 35 to 40
minutes

Pitted sour fresh frozen pie cherries should be
used. Taste cherries for sweetness more sugar may
be needed. If cherries are frozen with sugar a little
less may be needed.

When in Los Angeles Twin Peaks Cherry Pies
can be found at DuPars Restaurant and Bakery.

PIE CRUST

1 1/2 cups Flour
1/2 cup Crisco (lard)

Mix flour and Crisco together with a fork. When the
mixture takes on the appearance of little peas, add:

1/4 cup ice water

Mix together by hand. When sufficiently blended, roll
into ball and refrigerate over night. To roll out — flour
both your rolling pin and flat surface (marble is the
best, but if need be wax paper is a good substitute).
Split the ball into two. Roll out to fit pan and then roll
out second ball to use as lattice.

DOUBLE R DINER DAILY
SPECIALS FOR THE WEEK

Monday:
  Soup: Rabbit Bisque
  Entree: Liver and
  onions w/choice of
  vegetable and cup of
  soup or dinner salad.
  Coffee

Tuesday:
  Soup: Vegetable-
  Noodle
  Entree: Ham steak w/
  pineapple ring choice
  of vegetable (2) and
  cup of soup or dinner
  salad.
  Coffee

Wednesday:
  Soup: Beaver Barley
  Entree: Roast turkey w/
  all the fixins and cup
  of soup or dinner
  salad.
  Coffee

Dining

Thursday:
  Soup: Split Pea
  Entree: Lamb chops w/
  mint jelly or apple-
  sauce, vegetable (2)
  and cup of soup or
  dinner salad.
  Coffee

Friday:
  Soup: Corn Chowder or
  New England Clam
  Chowder
  Entree: Fish sticks with
  tartar sauce and
  vegetable (2) and
  choice of cup of soup
  or dinner salad.
  Coffee

Saturday:
  Soup: Cream of
  Huckleberry
  Entree: Cheeseburger
  w/fries and cup of
  soup or dinner salad.
  Coffee

Sunday:
  Leftovers
  Iced Tea

Doughnuts

Here in Twin Peaks, doughnuts are as much a part of our morning as a cup of good strong coffee and the *Twin Peaks Gazette*. Some say our sheriff started the current craze—he's been know to toss a half-dozen at a time. Some say it all started with the bake-off at the 1985 state fair, when **Mrs. Howard**'s doughnuts won a blue ribbon. The fact is that whether plump and filled, or white-sugared and crumbly, doughnuts have been a favored treat since the Dutch first fried up a batch of olykoeks in old New Amsterdam. Three years ago, in 1988, the estimated per capita doughnut consumption in Twin Peaks was 306—we'll venture a guess that is more doughnuts for every man, woman, and child than just about anywhere else in the U.S.

DOUGHNUT CAPITOL

Twin Peaks proudly boasts its consumption of more doughnuts per capita than any city, town or municipality in the world. Oil boiling from midnight to 6AM every day except Sunday, at the Wagon Wheel Bakery, **owned and operated by** June **and** Howard Wagner, **produces more than 1200 doughnuts and doughnut holes each shift. No one knows why its called**

Wagon Wheel; **maybe Howard wishes he were. Anyway, get there and get there fast because** June **and** Howard **are not getting younger (alas, not a child between them. The nieces and nephews are only interested in the money and no one in town likes them).** June **is from New Orleans and** Howard**'s from the Bronx; their doughnuts are a culture clash between beignets and bagels, the glorious result of a misunderstanding they had on their wedding night. Luckily they got busy slinging flour and we get the scrum-dilly-umptious results. Don't forget to ask for the holes, too.**

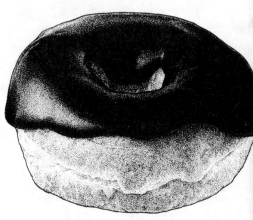

It is said that the circular doughnut evolved because the pearl ash widely used in America was not as efficient as yeast in raising the dough, and so left a soggy center—a problem easily solved by simply removing it ahead of time before frying. But all we can be sure of is that as the confection traveled west with the frontier, the wheel shape developed. Perhaps it was simply easier for the trail cook to roll out a little rope of dough between his hands and loop it into a circle so it would lie flat in the pan and require less fat to fry.

Be sure to stop by the **Double R Diner** for an early breakfast. Ask Norma for the Doughnut Special. Or if you're visiting the sheriff, see if you can snatch a couple off his desk when his back is turned. But know that every time you bite into a doughnut in Twin Peaks you're biting into a doughnut from the **Wagon Wheel Bakery**.

Doughnuts for 106

Chocolate doughnuts **go best with coffee, so here's the recipe, forthwith.**

Mix 3 1/2 cups of melted/cooled shortening, 6 2/3 cups of sugar and 16 jumbo eggs. Thoroughly fold in 6 generous cups of buttermilk. Sift in 29 cups of flour, 5 cups of unsweetened cocoa powder, 6 2/3 tablespoons of double-acting baking powder, 2 1/3 tablespoons of baking soda and 2 tablespoons of salt. Knead the dough on a lightly-floured surface until smooth. Roll the dough out to 1/2 inch thick and cut out doughnuts with a 2 1/2 inch doughnut cutter. Put doughnuts and holes

Dining

aside on wax paper. Heat about 2 inches of oil in a kettle until 375°, and drop in doughnuts a few at a time. Turn them as they rise, and cook each about 2-3 minutes. Scoop done doughnuts out with a slotted spoon and drain them on paper towels.

Glaze: **Melt 12 ounces of unsweetened chocolate with 2 1/2 cups of water over a double boiler, stirring smooth. Remove from heat and whisk in 10 pounds of powdered sugar. Dip tops of warm doughnuts in glaze and cool on racks.**

NORMA JENNINGS—Born September 30, 1950. After graduating from Twin Peaks Community College with a degree in Home Ec., Libra Norma travelled extensively in search of new and exotic recipes for meatloaf. Aghast at the unimaginative approaches taken to this uniquely American concoction, she opened the Double R Diner where

the meatloaf served is hallucinatory. A former Miss Twin Peaks ('69) and TPCC Small Business Owner of the Year, Norma is most at home in her diner talking with Big Ed. She believes in longer prison terms.

BESTS: "The people here, their warmth and sincerity." Also, the Timber players version of *The Paranormal Review*.

Jukebox selections at the Double R Diner page 83

Particularly essential to the Twin Peaks experience is the **Double R Diner** on Highway J (555-0087). No place else in town serves you two eggs, orange juice from concentrate, Beaver fritters and toast for $1.99.

Of course, with every meal comes delicious, FBI approved, coffee from the old, always reliable, J.H. McKie coffee maker.

Seats in each booth are upholstered in attractive and comfortable, stain-resistant vinyl and on every table are salt and pepper shakers, sugar, creamer (always fresh and full), ketchup, mustard, napkin dispenser and an ashtray. Diners sitting at the counter enjoy the same thoughtful amenities.

Service is attentive and courteous. **Norma Jennings** is dedicated to running a good old-fashioned diner, much to our good fortune. **Special Agent Cooper** put her cherry pie on the taste treat map where it belongs. And if you're lucky enough to be in town when blackberries are in season, **Norma**'s cobbler is divine. Her pie crust could win a bake-off. And the banana cream pie with snowy peaks of meringue piled on top has sent many a traveler to the motel to spend the night so they can come back for more. The Susie-Q's (skinny, curly french fries) are very popular among our local high school students. So much so that cheerleaders are advised against partaking. (A moment on the lips, forever on the hips.)

As you leave, note the sincere message on the front door:

THANKS WE APPRECIATE YOUR **PATRONAGE** **HAVE A NICE DAY** **PLEASE CALL AGAIN**

Everyone does!

A1	Working Man *John Conlee*	**W2**	I Want to Know You *Conway Twitty*	**M4**	Always On My Mind *Pet Shop Boys*
B1	Radio Lover	**X2**	Snake Boots	**N4**	Do I Have To
C1	Told A Lie To My Heart *W. Nelson & H. Williams, Jr.*	**Y2**	Shattered Dreams *Johnny Hates Jazz*	**O4**	No Mistake, She's Mine *K. Rogers & R. Milsap*
D1	Slow Movin' Outlaw	**Z2**	My Secret Garden	**P4**	You're My Love
E1	Little Lie *Fleetwood Mac*	**AA2**	Dirty Diana *Michael Jackson*	**Q4**	Songbird *Kenny G*
F1	Ricky	**BB2**	Instrumental	**R4**	Midnight Motion
G1	Stop Dragging My Heart *Stevie Nicks & Tom Petty*	**CC2**	Circle in the Sand *Belinda Carlisle*	**S4**	Are you Still In Love *Anne Murray*
H1	Kind of Woman	**DD2**	We Can Change	**T4**	Give Me Your Love
I1	Some Girls Have All *Louise Mandrell*	**EE2**	She's Like the Wind *Patrick Swayze*	**U4**	Can't We Try *D. Hill & Vonda Shepard*
J1	How Did I Get It So Late	**FF2**	Stay	**V4**	Pleasure Centre
K1	Save the Last Dance For Me *Dolly Parton*	**A3**	An Innocent Man *Billy Joel*	**W4**	Crazy *Patsy Cline*
L1	Elusive Butterfly	**B3**	I'll Cry Instead	**X4**	Your Cheatin' Heart
M1	Your Memory Ain't *Mickey Gilley*	**C3**	Need You Tonight *INXS*	**Y4**	Get Outta My Dreams *Billy Ocean*
N1	Lonely Nights	**D3**	I'm Coming Home	**Z4**	Showdown
O1	There's No Way *Alabama*	**E3**	Never Gonna Give U up *Rick Astley*	**AA4**	Kentucky Rain *Elvis Presley*
P1	The Boy	**F3**	Instrumental	**BB4**	My Little Friend
Q1	Human Touch *Rick Springfield*	**G3**	So Emotional *Whitney Houston*	**CC4**	Proud Mary *Credence Clearwater*
R1	Alyson	**H3**	For the Love of You	**DD4**	Born in the Bayou
S1	Me and Paul *Willie Nelson*	**I3**	Valley Road *Bruce Hornsby*	**EE4**	Sweet Dreams *Patsy Cline*
T1	I Let My Mind Wander	**J3**	Long Race	**FF4**	Blue Moon of Kentucky
U1	Hurts So Good *John Cougar*	**K3**	Your Heart Desires *Hall and Oates*	**A5**	Just to See Her *Smokey Robinson*
V1	Close Enough	**L3**	Realove	**B5**	I'm Gonna Love You
W1	The Lady in Red *Chris de Burgh*	**M3**	I Wanna Dance with U *Eddie Rabbit*	**C5**	Who Wears These Shoes *Elton John*
X1	The Vision	**N3**	Gotta Have You	**D5**	Sad Song
Y1	When Giving Up Was Easy *Ed Bruce*	**O3**	Baby Blue *George Strait*	**E5**	All I Want Is You *Carly Simon*
Z1	Texas Girl	**P3**	Back to Bein' Me	**F5**	Two Hot Girls
AA1	Part Time Lover *Stevie Wonder*	**Q3**	Night Shift *Commodores*		
BB1	Instrumental	**R3**	I Keep Running		**Dining**
CC1	Longhaired Redneck *David Allan Coe*	**S3**	Back in the USSR *Billy Joel*	**G5**	It Takes A Little Rain *Oak Ridge Boys*
DD1	U Never Call My Name	**T3**	Big Shot	**H5**	Looking for Love
EE1	Good-Bye Marie *Kenny Rogers*	**U3**	Stand By Me *Ben E. King*	**I5**	Take My Breath Away *Berlin*
FF1	Abraham, Martin and John	**V3**	Yakety Yak	**J5**	Radar Radio
A2	Mountain Dew *Willie Nelson*	**W3**	Out Goin' Cattin' *Sawyer Brown*	**K5**	I Know Where I'm Going *The Judds*
B2	Laying My Burdens Down	**X3**	The House Won't Rock	**L5**	If I Were You
C2	I'm For Love *Hank Williams, Jr.*	**Y3**	Nothings Gonna Stay Us *Starship*	**M5**	80's Ladies *K. T. Olsin*
D2	Lawyers, Guns and Money	**Z3**	Laying It On the Line	**N5**	Old Picture
E2	Just a Giggolo *David Lee Roth*	**AA3**	Legs *ZZ Top*	**O5**	Sexy Girl *Glenn Fry*
F2	I Don't Got Nobody	**BB3**	Sharp Dressed Man	**P5**	USA
G2	Take me Down *Alabama*	**CC3**	Dancing in the Dark *Bruce Springstein*	**Q5**	What Friends Are For *Dionne Warwick & Friends*
H2	Lovin' You	**DD3**	Pink Cadillac	**R5**	Two Ships Passing
I2	You're Only Human *Billy Joel*	**EE3**	What's Love Got to Do With It *Tina Turner*	**S5**	We're In the Love *Al Jarreau*
J2	Surprises	**FF3**	Rock and Roll Widow	**T5**	Breakin' Away
K2	Rock and Roll Girls *John Fogerty*	**A4**	U Never Find Another *Lou Rawls*	**U5**	When Going Gets Tough *Billy Ocean*
L2	Centerfold	**B4**	Let's Fall in Love	**V5**	Instrumental
M2	I Found Someone *Cher*	**C4**	Do Ya *K. T. Olsin*	**W5**	I Wanna Dance *Whitney Houston*
N2	Dangerous Times	**D4**	Lonely But Only For U	**X5**	Moment of Truth
O2	Love Don't Give Reason *Smokey Robinson*	**E4**	Can Do the Heartbreak *Anne Murray*	**Y5**	Shine, Shine, Shine *Eddy Raven*
P2	Hanging On By A Thread	**F4**	Without You	**Z5**	Stay With Me
Q2	Captain of Her Heart *Double*	**G4**	Seven Spanish Angels *W. Nelson & R. Charles*	**AA5**	Way You Make Me Feel *Michael Jackson*
R2	Your Prayer Takes Me	**H4**	Who Cares	**BB5**	Instrumental
S2	Can't Stay Away From You *Miami Sound Machine*	**I4**	Fallin' Again! *Alabama*	**CC5**	Ain't Misbehavin' *Hank Williams, Jr.*
T2	Let It Loose	**J4**	Saw the Time	**DD5**	I've Been Around
U2	Deep River Woman *Lionel Richie*	**K4**	Words Get in the Way *Miami Sound Machine*	**EE5**	Just Enough Love *Ray Price*
V2	Ballerina Girl	**L4**	Movies	**FF5**	Why Don't Love Go Away

Eileen Hayward's Coffee for a Crowd

(40 to 250 servings)

Eileen always makes this for the annual spring luncheon put on by the Ladies Auxiliary to benefit children in Lower Town.

1 large cheesecloth bag
1 pound coffee
6 eggshells (freeze the yolks and whites for future use)
1/2 cup chicory
5-7 quarts well water (tap water is okay)

Place grounds and egg shells in the cheesecloth bag. In a large kettle,

Dining

bring the water to a boil. Place the filled cheesecloth bag in the kettle (fire is turned off). Let stand on the stove for 10 minutes (stir the bag several times). Remove bag. Serve immediately.

Bottoms up!

DINING OUT IN TWIN PEAKS

If you want to give yourself a present make a reservation at the **Timber Room** in the **Great Northern Hotel** or the **Lamplighter Inn**; you'll have a meal to remember, and enjoy mingling with the fine people of Twin Peaks. **Sheriff Truman** could easily be at the next table, and **Doc Hayward** doesn't like the sun to set on Sunday without feasting on the Eggs Sardou.

Breakfast caters to the hale and hardy, particularly if you're going hiking or hunting. But for those more delicate appetites the homemade granola is outstanding. And don't miss the freshly baked Banana Nut Muffins.

Lunch is popular with our local businessmen, all of whom rave about the Chili. The soups are always good and the **Croque Monsieur** melts in your mouth. (It's spelled "Croaked" Monsieur on the menu in honor of Dougie Milford who especially loved it, and who has indeed gone on to his higher reward.)

Dinner is a culinary adventure, depending on whether or not **Jerry Horne** is in residence. He travels the world in search of bizarre and wonderful taste bud ticklers. But if you're not in the mood for the *outre*, stick to the tried and true—stuffed baked dove, braised venison, fried rabbit, and wild roast

JAMES HURLEY— **January 1, 1973. The quiet, inner strength of this Capricorn is truly remarkable. Coming from a broken home,** James **concluded pretty early on that people can seldom be trusted which is why he's perplexed so many people trust him. With his Harley and the open road he is fulfilled.**

luck with brown rice. The garlic cheese grits are a must. Poems have been written in tribute. The biscuits are skillet baked and are best when eaten with sorghum molasses. The wine list is varied and excellent, again thanks to brother **Jerry**. Request the Croatian Beaujolais, or order a Bull Shot from the bar. A good savory time will be had by all!

South of Twin Peaks on Highway 21, near Lewis Fork, is the **Lamplighter Inn** (555-2829), a rustic establishment designed with nubby colors that make you feel right at home. The chicken pot pies are close to celestial. For lunch, Agent Cooper recommends, "a tuna fish sandwich on whole wheat and a slice of cherry pie and coffee. Damn good food."

Other fun food spots are **Angelo Wong's** Italian/ Thai restaurant, at 77 Main St. (555-7823). The food is too delicious to describe. (**Jerry Horne** loves it.) **Ace's Bar-B-Que** located at 44 So. Lynch Rd (555-4550) is also a good bet. His ribs are tender, and a lot of visitors buy the sauce for Christmas presents. It's a good idea to inquire what the specialty of the day is—in case it's barbecued goat. (Not recommended for the squeamish.) And the **Roadhouse** located on Highway J (555-1919) is always good for a corn dog if you've missed dinner every place else. But it's the frosty mugs and the cold brew that draws their crowd. This is definitely the place to enjoy our local night owls.

Lodging

BESTS: His uncle Ed, Route 21 north of White Tail Falls at around 3AM on his Harley, Julee Cruise at the Roadhouse.

TRUDY CHELGREN
GREAT NORTHERN
EMPLOYEE OF THE YEAR

QUOTE: The customer is always right and so is the wine glass.

Practically everybody's favorite waitress in the Great Northern Timber Room, Trudy Chelgren finished first in the employee's poll for this year's award.

Ben Horne says, "I think what makes Trudy so spe-

Lodging

cial is that her smile never leaves her face and everyone who comes into the Timber Room notices that and feels special, too."

Trudy is a native of Twin Peaks. In fact, she is a former assistant captain of the Steeplejack cheerleading squad and Morale Officer of the Bridge Club.

She also hosts one of the more fun events of the year here in town. Being an avid shutterbug, every spring she invites folks over to look at hundreds of slides of the many colorful awnings that seem to flourish in our town.

Continued margin
page 89

GREAT NORTHERN HOTEL

The most elegant and complete accommodations in Twin Peaks are found here. Available are 102 beautifully appointed rooms, each personalized and panelled in comforting **Ponderosa Pine** from our own **Packard Mill**. Several elegant suites are available besides rooms for singles, couples and larger configurations. (Take a peek at the Honeymoon Suite and feast your eyes). Breakfast, lunch and dinner are available in the **Timber Room** as well as through room service, and picnic lunches can be ordered for your pleasure while touring the surrounding local beauty. $$$. Excellent coffee. Located at 500 Great Northern Highway. 1-800-555-1000. Accepts all major credit cards.

LeAnn's Country Inn
315 Timber Lane
Twin Peaks WA 99153
555-2487

Amble down a country lane to a charming Victorian surrounded by spacious gardens. Relax in front of a crackling fire, or take the air on an old-fashioned porch swing. Queen-size beds, private baths, Continental breakfast, and a complimentary copy of the *Twin Peaks Gazette*.

Snow Street Inn
552 Snow Street
Twin Peaks WA 99153
555-7653

Six lavishly furnished guest rooms, each with private bath, balcony, and fireplace. A gourmet breakfast is served every morning. Bicycles, mopeds, hammocks. Swimming nearby at Pearl Lakes.

The Willow Inn
123 Snow Street
Twin Peaks WA 99153
555-8980

A remodeled Victorian tucked away on seven acres of woodland. Tennis court, swimming pool, bicycles, fishing equipment. Each of the eight rooms has a private bath, working fireplace, and a brass bed. Continental breakfast and afternoon refreshments. Just a five-minute walk from Timber Place, Twin Peaks' summer stock theater.

Pine View Motel: What it lacks in elegance it makes up for in courtesy and privacy. Assignations can be scheduled here without fear of being compromised. Continental breakfast of juice, coffee, fruit, doughnuts are available. And since you're a stone's throw from the **Double R Diner** you simply have to pop down the street for a delicious meal. 16 units. $$. Avoid the coffee. Located at 1289 Highway J. 555-PINE. Accepts M.C., V. Minimum 4 hour stay.

The Cozy Box Bed 'N Breakfast Locally know as The Coze. It's right in the center of town, in a fine Victorian home (Originally owned by the Martell's until Nealith lost it in a poker game—the only one he ever played.) Convenient to all shops and restaurants. The rooms have themes to fit your every mood; English Country, Hall of Mirrors, Wizard of Oz, Santa Fe, Laplander, Little Bo-Peep and 1001 Nights. There's a hot tub. **Irene** and **Loomis Peterson** are the proud proprietors, and they serve wine and cheese to tubbers during the cocktail hour. The breakfast portion comes from **Wagon Wheel Bakery** so you can kill two birds with one stone by staying here. Seven units. $$. Coffee is pretty good, when you can get it. Located at 244 Enthwhistle St. 555-4842. Cash only.

Mrs. Thrimble's Bed and Breakfast Located on Sparkwood Road several hundred yards after the pavement turns into dirt (or, in the spring, mud) **Emma Thrimble** opened her roomy if drafty home to travellers in the early 1950's and has been bedding and boarding visitors ever since. Five rooms are available. Reservations should be made. Breakfast, lunch and dinner are served in Emma's kitchen. Plop down $1.00 for breakfast, $2.50 for lunch and $3.00 for dinner. Grab a plate and wander into the kitchen where anything on the stove is for you. 5 Units. $. Coffee is pretty good. Located at 29 So. Sparkwood Rd., in Lower town. 555-1800. Cash or personal checks with photo identification.

(continued)
An international traveler in her youth, it seems appropriate that she is in the Twin Peaks United Nations Choir **as the first soprano.**

A great piece of wood was presented to Trudy in a swell ceremony in Ben Horne**'s office. On the wood were these words:**

"There's always a tune with the toast. A few notes with the noodles. A ditty for dessert. She's the gal who will always sing for your supper with a song in her head and a plate in her hand. She's the sweetheart of the Timber Room."

(Over 48 dollars were raised to have all these wonderful sentiments burnt into wood.)

Lodging

Great Northern Lobby floor plan

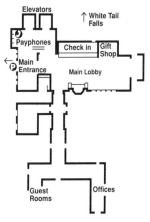

89

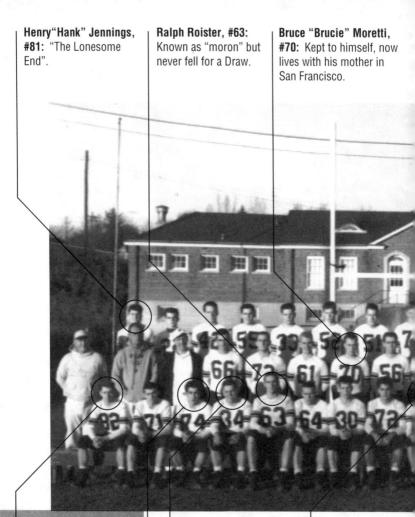

Henry"Hank" Jennings, #81: "The Lonesome End".

Ralph Roister, #63: Known as "moron" but never fell for a Draw.

Bruce "Brucie" Moretti, #70: Kept to himself, now lives with his mother in San Francisco.

Samuel Diefenderfer, #82: "Be-bop-a-lula, she's my baby", Married Mary Witherspoon and disappeared.

Albert "The Muff" Furrer, #34: A very fuzzy thinker when they called the plays, and especially when it came to girls.

Harry S. Truman, #1 Quarterback—best completion record in the Tri-County Area fo two straight seasons.

Tommy "The Hawk" Hill, #74: Halfback; "Hero of the Undefeated Season".

BOBO HOBSON— "Coach **has never been photographed, convinced that each developed image on film robs one of a part of their soul. He has, however, coached the Steeplejacks to three State Semi-Finals in the last five years. A Virgo, though he won't admit it,**

Continued margin page 91

TWIN PEAKS FOOTBALL TEAM PICTURE:

ROW #1: (left to right) Samuel Diefenderfer, Kenny Wilson, Tommy Hill, Albert Furrer, Ralph Roister, John Johnson, Jeff Hurley, Tony Bacci, Harry Truman, Ed Hurley, Steve Farkel, Don Pinkle, Tim Simons, Stan Lillas, Ted Bjornborg, Mike Reevo, Joe Hastings, Skip Lippertz.
ROW #2: Coach Bellis, Chaplain "Uncle Walt" Barnhardt, Trainer: Herb Frederick, Lance Masterlund, Mac Fousteck, Earle Black, Sam Miller, Lester Arnholdt,

Herb "Cutthroat" Sear, #67: Sidelined 7 quarterbacks in the season. Favorite saying "Let's kick some essence of butt."

Mannie "Schnozola" Josephson, #53: Best sense of humor; always knew the punchline but never 'read' a play.

Thadilonius "Toad" Barker, #12: Known as the roving defensive back.

"Big Ed" Hurley, #60: Stopped 'em cold almost every time.

Phil "Hashbrowns" Mazlowski, #50: Tough on the front line, even tougher on his underwear.

Greg "Goat" Latroit: "Father to Everybody", but still the Student Trainer.

I'm a jack and you're a jack
Steeple jacks are we
And when we get together
The cry is "Victory"!
   The Steeplejack Cheer

Henry Houlanan, Matt Stewart, Bruce Moretti, Richard Epsen, Colby Baker, Mike Greeby, Philip Fitzgerald, Gary Swyker, Asst. Coaches Bill Chapman, Gene Pamloski, Bill Conway.

ROW #3: Stu Grefendorfer, Jim Jacoby, David Tremayne, Dennis Rohrer, Gary Leicht, Casper Frey, Vince Brennan, Toby Markle, Bill Shear, Phil Mazlowski, Mannie Josephson, Thadilonius Barker, Greg Franchea, Dave Rrattichett, Mark Bartlett, Mickey Koontz, Sam Herd.

(continued)
Coach **teaches business skills and computer programming at the high school and says," If you can't kick, don't bother."**

BESTS: Fall in Twin Peaks, Caribou Festival, dropping a clean log in the woods.

"Nobody beat us. Nobody."

From the Pearl Lakes to Snake River..
From Seattle to distant Rome...
We must always love and cherish...
Our High School and our Home.

- Twin Peaks Alma Mater

Football carries a long tradition in Twin Peaks. The first forward pass in the great northwest was thrown by then-high school freshman, **Mayor Dwayne Milford**, who took the ball from the center and lofted it over four yards to his brother **Dougie**, who, unfortunately fell over. But nevertheless, the first forward pass in the great northwest was thrown, and from the playing fields of Eaton to the Kingdom, football would never be the same.

And that's something that has made the town proud since November of 1968, when that grand football season ended. Champions of the **Northwest Nine Conference** and **State Champs** duly elected by the **Seattle Football Outing** and **Auning Association**.

Many of the stars of the team have stayed in town and went on to useful careers including **Sheriff Truman, Deputy Hawk, Ed Hurley** and **Hank Jennings**. **Truman**'s gait reminded many of the experts of **Crazy Leg Hirsch**. **Big Ed**, on the other hand, was said to be the next **Leon Hart Tommy "the Hawk" Hill**. **Hawk** baffled most experts—too small for defense, too slow for offense, yet he got the goddamn job done. "He was the kind of guy you would like to have next to you in a fox hole" was how **Coach Hobson** described him.

THE SEASON

The schedule suggested that the tough games were at the beginning of the season. How far they were from the truth...

GAME ONE 14-13

The season got off to a slow but exciting start. Looking back on it, you could even call it scary; a 14-13 squeaker over Metaline at home.

Leading 13 to 7, Metaline inexplicably tried the old "fumble ruskie" and **Hank Jennings**, employing some sort of sixth sense—an ability he never put to much use in later life—sensed chicanery. He grabbed the ball in mid air and waltzed untouched 87 yards to a touchdown. "We knew we were into something good", said the team's star quarterback, **Sheriff Harry Truman.**

GAME TWO 48-46

Northport fell under the Steeplejack juggernaut 48 - 46 in one of the wildest games the town has ever seen. When, three years later, **Northport High School** was tossed out of the **Northwest Nine**, it was learned that they had hired grown men to play athletics for them. As **Tommy "The Hawk"** put it, "There was one guy who I had bought a car from the month before."

GAME THREE 38-0

The **Steeplejacks** played the game in the dark at Colville when the lights went out and both teams elected to continue. It was unfortunate for Colville, which featured a stunning passing attack. The game was called with the Jacks ahead 38 to 0.

In this game, the **Steeplejacks** added a new feature—the Lonesome half-back. The gifted but troubled, **Hank Jennings** refused to practice and eventually refused to join the huddle. *But he could run!* Easily the most gifted of the team, but with an attitude that bordered on anti-social. **Hank** would stand six or seven yards away from the huddle and wait for the team to come to the line of scrimmage. Then, through an elaborate set of hand signals from the head of the Science and Industry Club, who was receiving the plays from **Coach Hobson**'s son, **Sammy.** Hank would be given the play.

The effect, of course, was mesmerizing and brilliantly effective. Most of the time **Hank** was unstoppable.

THE TIE 2-2

As the team boarded the bus for Evan, the news hit like a ton of lead. **Hank Jennings** had been suspended. "No one ever knew why, but the team stood behind the Coach." Most accounts of why are unclear. Yelling was heard in the coaches' office, and then a window broke, and then the words no football competitor ever wants to hear pierced the air— "You're benched."

Then the rain started. Rain that finished destroyed most farms in the vicinity. Needless to say, playing football in it was a tragedy. And without **Hank**, the offense could do nothing more than punt. 16 times to be exact. And like some biblical story in the bible, it felt decreed. There would be no winner or loser that day.

Returning home **Coach Hobson** was met by angry Steeplejack supporters who demanded to know why he left **Hank** out of the game. "the damn rain..." was all he would ever say. Till the day he died, it was simply, "The damn rain." He had too much class to lay it off to one of his boys, no matter the problem.

GAME FOUR 33-23

It was supposed to be the easiest game of the year, but no one counted on **Cliff "The Combine" Ompehunt** failing for a third time to graduate from Knife River High. He ran wild—until he was injured. It happened in a pileup near the end zone. **Hank Jennings** had made the tackle and as he told a reporter later, "**Ompehunt** must have spiked himself—bad." From then on it was all Twin Peaks. They scored at will and pulled out a 33 to 23 victory.

GAME FIVE 13-3

It was an uneventful victory at Marcus other than the fact that the team's student manager, **Herb Fredrick**, left most of the school's uniforms at the dentist and the game started an hour and a half late.

GAME SIX 18-12

The longest road trip of the year: all the way to Chewelah. A game so cold that it was the one and only time anyone ever, and they mean ever, heard leader **Coach Hobson** use the Lord's name in vain. Well not really in vain, most specifically he was asking the Lord above to warm things up a bit.

The highlight of this game illustrates just what kind of Coach Hobson was. He gathered the team in the locker room. Everyone seemed tense and unsure of themselves. Then, and this is what made him one of the great ones, he began to talk like **Knute Rockne**. It wasn't until years later that the team realized he was lip synching. As **Tommy "The Hawk"** said, "Who cared, for that moment I was a Golden Domer."

GAME SEVEN 19-0, GAME EIGHT 12-2

The next two wins came easily. Coasting on the all-too-accurate arm of **Sheriff Truman**, and the steady hands of **Big Ed Hurley.** The **Steeplejacks** looked unstoppable.

GAME NINE 9-3

And so it boiled down to that final game against Kettle Falls. And the **Steeplejacks** saved the best and most exciting for last.

For three quarters all either team could manage was a field goals. 3 to 3. As the final seconds ticked away, **Harry Truman** put together a scoring drive that will not soon be forgotten. Four short passes, a cross-buck lateral play, and three straight quarterback sneaks—the last one, going 41 yards, left the **Steeplejacks** on the Cougars' four yard line.

Sports

That was when inspiration struck **Tommy "the Hawk" Hill**. In **Sheriff Truman**'s words:

"He came into the huddle like a whole different guy. None of us knew what was going on and most of us were pretty darn scared. I remember he looked at me and he said, "There is special providence in the flight of the eagle. If it be now, let it be. If it be not now, let it be so." And then for a reason I will never know I said, "**Hawk**, take the ball and take us home." It wasn't until five years later that I learned **Hawk** had fallen and hit his head and was misquoting Shakespeare's "Hamlet" from a homework assignment.

COACH HOBSON

The coach's tombstone, which is visited by every Steeplejack team on the night before Homecoming reads, "There are no atheists on Fourth and long."

His other two favorite sayings were:

"The pigskin is nothing more than an inflated bladder, so lay off the booze boys."

"The goal post is in the shape of an H and that means Hell and that's what you have to go through to get some points."

His devotion to Knute Rockne **is evident. The dates on his tombstone are 1889 - 1937. The days** Rockne **entered and left his mortal coil.**

To his dying day Coach Hobson **insisted when**

writing about the championship season to always spell the team's record this way—Eight Oh and Won. **This often led to people asking him if somewhere in his background he was Chinese, but he remained undaunted.**

"The ball was snapped back to me and I gave it to **Hawk** who had never played in the backfield before. In an instant his once calm exterior melted into something akin to panic.

"HE BEGAN TO RUN THE WRONG WAY."

"We couldn't catch him and neither could they. He sprinted back to our five yard line and stopped either catching his breath or finally coming to his senses. I remember shouting to him about going the other way and he said something about life being a path and he started up-field.

"It was a beautiful thing to behold. Through what seemed to be a planned strategy he had completely strung out the Cougar defense and getting to the end zone was as easy as walking around a putt-putt course. The play took well over fifteen minutes but we were state champs and no one can ever take that away from us."

The headlines in the paper the next day read:

"MYSTERY PLAY SAVES PEAKS SEASON."

Little did they know.

"THE BEST THING IN OUR LIVES AND WE DID IT TOGETHER." was

how **Ed Hurley** described it. "We were Eight - 0 and 1. Nobody beat us. Nobody."

WHAT TO WEAR

We're not a snooty community, so whatever you're comfortable in is pretty much o.k. with us. Still, it's never a bad idea to look presentable and, in regards to this, **Mr. Richard Tremayne** is raising the consciousness of our town as well as the entire country about the varieties of ensembles possible in the area of Woodsy wear. The fashion center of Los Angeles, that hub of the *haute monde*, recently focused on our town in the world of fashion.

Fashion and Where to Get It

In a capricious world of passing fancies, short-lived fads of the *haute monde*, our citizens cling staunchly and with confidence to the tried-and-true, proven things that have withstood the 'test of time.' Nowhere is this more proudly exemplified than in the clothes we wear.

This is not to say Twin Peaks' citizens are conservative in their dress. Some of our most distinguished citizens are known and recognized for the flamboyance of their apparel and, recently, in his fashion show at **The Roadhouse, Mr. Richard Tremayne** demonstrated the varieties of subtle ensemble one can achieve with traditional dress and a little imagination. Nevertheless, while visiting our community you will feel most comfortable if you stick to A-line skirts or clean denim jeans, sensible pumps, simple blouses or crewneck sweaters, twill or wool pants (pleats optional), plaid shirts, cowboy boots or moccasins and a reasonable blazer (wear a double breasted and someone will think you're putting on airs).

Fashion

While our climate affects the types of apparel Peakers don, there is a strong tradition of aesthetics involved in our choices, too. This can be seen in the wide variety of fashionable but good items available at **Horne's Department Store** on Highway J. From the sensible blouses of cotton and silk in a variety of colors for women of discriminating taste to the rich and nubby plaid wool shirts for our virile men, Horne's is a one-stop shopping

center in our community. Also of interest is the perfume counter on the ground floor where international scents mingle.

For our working men and women who require sturdy apparel, durable boots and who wouldn't be caught dead in bikini briefs, **Ed Strimble's Worker's Warehouse** at 52 Cedar St. carries a

Locals

large selection of denim jeans and coveralls, twill work pants, steel-toed and calked boots and wool shirts for industrial use. **Ed** also carries a complete line of uniforms for our municipal employees.

Fashion

Besides being down-to-earth in their tastes, our citizens are also industrious; many of the attractive skirts and jackets you see around town are home-made. For a superb selection of fabrics in myriad colors and patterns from silk to sateen, **Gentle-man Jim's** directly down the street from Horne's at Highway J is a must. If you're sewing anything—from culottes to curtains—this fabric emporium will be a funhouse for you.

For something a little different, stop into **Carlson's Odd Shop**, 300 Old Mill Rd. **Art** and **Emma Carlson** have on display a wide and fascinating variety of authentic, handmade brooches, earrings, tie-clasps and what-nots fashioned by native

Amerindians from soapstone, lapis lazuli, agate, **Ponderosa Pine** and other natural materials. A brief chat with either **Emma** or **Art** will inform you how their shop got its name.

And if you're wondering where **Dr. Jacoby** gets his colorful shirts, well, we asked him. "Mail order," he told us. "From Hawaii."

Locals

FURNITURE

A burl table, saw lamp and adz-hewn loveseat—these are things of beauty, grace and strength, and, like so many of the fine furniture pieces in and around Twin Peaks, they have found niches in the History of Design Art as the first truly "found objects." The desire to recapitulate indoors what is loved outdoors prods Twin Peakers to seek out unusual shapes in nature, sit in them or eat food off them or simply gaze at their rugged heft by the light of a fire from the hearth. After all, it's only natural. And a lot less expensive than Eames chairs and Swedish designer stuff.

A spiritually-minded community, Twin Peaks supports a number of churches representing the world's major religions as well as a few sort of 'iffy' ones.

Lutheran. On Sparkwood, south of the Great Northern Road is the **Church of the Good Sheperd**, a congregation of the Missouri Synod with membership made up of many prominent families such as the **Palmers**, **Briggs** and **Jennings**. **Pastor Theodore Helmark** leads the congregation in Sunday Services at 9:45AM and 11:00AM. Sunday School at 11:00AM. Coffee and doughnuts served in the annex after service. Knowledge of the Nicene Creed required for membership although tourists and transients are tolerated. 59 Church Lane. 555-LUTH.

St. Hubert saw the crucifix between the antlers of a stag. He's a favorite around Twin Peaks.

Catholic. **Christ the King** is a 1/2 mile north of **Big Ed's Gas Farm** and cannot be missed because it is the only church in Twin Peaks built entirely of stone and displays a breathtaking Rose window intersected by delicate **Douglas Fir** mullions. Construction financed primarily through the **Packard Mill**. Membership includes the **Hurleys**, **Polaskis** and **Packards**. **Father Dunne** and **Brother Poplinski** celebrate Mass at 8:30AM, 9:30AM, 10:30AM, 11:30AM and 5:45PM Sun.; 7:45PM Tuesday and Thurs.; 5:30PM Fri.; Communion at 11:30AM and 5:45PM Sun. and 5:30PM Fri.; Confession is round-the-clock. Bring your own coffee. Corner of Church Lane and Thrasher Ave. 555-3333.

Baptist. **The Third Baptist Church of Black Lake** worships in a nondescript, one-room clapboard shack that began as a two-seater on Highway J 1/2 mile east of **the Log Lady**'s house. Ministers leading the flock in Sunday prayer are either **Nathan Quilp** or **Oliver Twist**. Service times vary, though you can arrive between 10:00AM and noon on Sunday and be sure someone will show up. Dancing, card playing and drinking are prohibited. Coffee—4 stars—when available. 89 Tony Ave. 555-LORD.

Episcopal. **Twin Peaks Episcopal** crowns **Meadowlark Hill** like a monument and from the cleanly-wrought belltower of **Douglas Fir** (financed by **Horne's Department Store**) can be seen **White Tail Falls**, the **Great Northern Lodge**, almost all of **Black Lake** and **Horne's Department Store**. **Reverend Clarence Brocklehurst** leads Sunday Services at 9:30AM and 11:00AM. Day Care is available. Punctuality is required though you don't have to be particularly devout. Prominent in the congregation are the **Haywards** and **Hornes**. Coffee is available, but it's expensive. 15 North Western St. 555-2222.

Other. **Twin Peaks Theosophist Society** meets somewhere around Twin Peaks (always outdoors) every third Wednesday following the New Moon except when there is a Blue Moon, at which time the society skips a service and holds, instead, an *eisteddvodai* or Poetry Blow-out just this side of the Canadian border on the shore of **Black Lake**. Committed to revelation of divine principles and first causes, the society has had as members **Pete Martel** and the **Log Lady**. Rumors circulated that **Agent Dale Cooper** once attended but the FBI denies this. Coffee is out of thermoses and is usually tepid if not cold. Telephone number is unlisted.

Circulars: the completed circle

A small tribe consisting of perhaps fifty to sixty-two members, the Circulars believed in the Cyclical/Circular nature of existence; what is given returns to the giver. Hence, the name Circular. By eating the flesh of fellow humans, the Circulars believed they could assume the nobler aspects of their victims, although reports suggest that in some instances loathsome characteristics were assumed [*see*: Potter, J. *Fear and Loathing in Early Black Lake Tribes*. TP Press, 1979]. To insure against being eaten themselves, the Circulars smeared elk feces over their bodies, making their flesh inedible and their tribe understandably lonesome.

Religious Worship

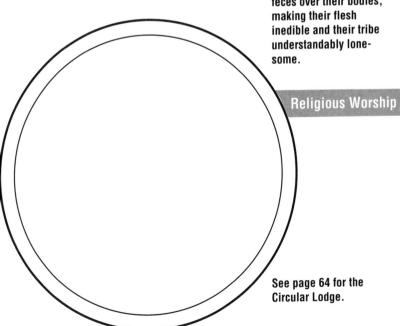

See page 64 for the Circular Lodge.

Radio Stations

KSNM (89.9 FM)
Country/western most of the time but carries NPR 'All Things Considered' every evening at 5PM. 555-KSNM

KILL (63.5 AM)
Timber news and weather conditions as well as school and social function cancellations. DJs Ned Buntline **and** Annie Bjornstrom, **announce the time and weather forecast hourly. Comedy Hour every Friday at 7:00PM features comics such as** "Olson and Johnson", "Lord Buckley" **and replays of** "Amos 'n' Andy". **Also announces daily 'specials' at the** Double R Diner. **555-KILL**

Received in Twin Peaks

KBOP (1157 AM)
Classic Rock from Spokane.
In bad weather, forget it.
KLON (98.5 AM)
From Loon Lake **down south of us. No regular broadcasting hours; reception iffy. A peculiar mixture of Creole and Cajun recipes peppered with authentic Blue Grass music from pirate labels.**
CBCC **(105.3 FM)**
CBC Radio Canada out of Calgary, Alberta. French spoken most of the time.

Transportation

Classical music and popular if melancholy French ballads. Shuts down at 1:00 a.m.

Television Stations
Unless you've got a satellite dish, forget it.

Getting to Twin Peaks is a little easier than getting out of it, though not half so difficult as getting around in it.

Since the Northern Pacific Spur ceased passenger operations out of Seattle in 1962, Trailways and Greyhound bus lines from Spokane are the most convenient and economical besides being pretty much the only game in town. Until the town council can finance the new bus hub, boarding and disembarking is in the parking lot out front of the **Double R Diner**.

Of course, travel to Twin Peaks by air is not at all difficult, just expensive, requiring a privately chartered small jet or a twin/single engine sort of thing. You may land and take off from the remaining landing strip at the old **Unguin Air Force Base**. Established in the late 1940's and named after **James Packard**'s wife, the base is 15 miles south of Twin Peaks. Call ahead for weather conditions (555-0004); Fred will be just as helpful as he possibly can.

Once you're here, getting around the town is somewhat more problematical. **Tom and Tim's Taxidermy and Taxi** [see page 58] is a little less than reliable but the brothers mean well. It helps to give them a little advance notice of a day or two. But they'll take you wherever you want to go, spice the trip with plenty of lore and charge you a reasonable fare. Tel. 555-TAXI.

BUS SCHEDULE *(Busses depart across from the Roadhouse)*

Local

#407 Dam Bus

	arr	dep	arr	dep	arr	dep	arr	dep
Twin Peaks		8:01		10:03		Noon		4:10
Black Lake Dam	8:23	8:25	10:25	10:30	12:30	12:35	4:40	4:45
Packard Sawmill	9:12	9:15	11:17	11:20	1:32	1:40	5:55	6:02
Kootenay Bay	10:45		12:50		4:05		7:35	

#3 Missoula Missile

	arr	dep	arr	dep	arr	dep	arr	dep
Twin Peaks		6:01		6:15		5:05		10:25
Coeur d'Alene	10:03	10:10	10:03	11:00	9:06	9:10	2:28	2:35
Kellogg	11:33	11:35	12:04	12:05	11:43	11:41	5:02	5:15
Missoula	2:37		2:38		2:42		8:17	

Interstate

West Coast Flyer (S)

	arr	dep
Twin Peaks		8:40
Portland	2:34	3:10
San Francisco	7:30	8:40
Hollywood	5:40	

West Coast Flyer (N)

	arr	dep
Hollywood		7:45
San Francisco	4:42	5:40
Spokane	9:47	10:00
Twin Peaks	4:46	

Eastern Express (E)

	arr	dep
Twin Peaks, WA		7:13
Philadelphia, PA	†8:40	9:30
New York, NY	11:47	12:40
B'hampton, LI, NY	2:32	

Pacific Woods Line (W)

	arr	dep
B'hampton, LI, NY		3:20
New York, NY	5:32	6:30
Philadelphia, PA	9:40	10:00
Twin Peaks, WA	‡8:40	

† 7 to 8 days later   ‡ 7 to 8 days later

Call Tim & Tom's Taxidermy 555-8238 for round-the-clock transportation almost anywhere. Reasonable rates. Discounts on wall-mounted trout available.

Volume 1, Number 1   *"Something is different."*   February, 1991

The Newspaper in a Smiling Bag Welcomes You

Twin Peaks is more than just a spot on the map. It's a spot on the mind. So when you step off your front porch in Miami, or wherever, and wonder where the pine trees went, just turn around, go back inside, and look in the *Gazette*. We're here, and really, so are you. If you live in Twin Peaks, you know it.

The connectedness of the Peak experience shared by the many regular viewers of the series bonds us into a community. We have been referred to by the press as a "cult following," but are we not simply neighbors? A casual channel-changer might mistake us for union extras, but no. Our union is a union of consciousness, one that stretches and flips as we walk that delicate, wavering edge together every Saturday night, bonded by more than city lines and common street corners.

A newspaper should mirror its community — no matter how abstract, no matter how troubled — with wit, compassion and clairvoyance. To that end, we invite you to consider this paper a forum for your ruminations, cognitions and general opinions. Please send any letters, stories, articles, philosophy, graphics, or insights that you'd like to share with your neighbors. Any unusual goings-on you may notice around town will also be appreciated. Selected contributions will be published here in the newspaper in a smiling bag. Help us overturn those large flat rocks of unawareness that surround us and be astounded at what comes writhing out from underneath.

Highlights of this first issue include an interview with Richard Beymer, an Audrey Horne look-alike photo contest, and the introduction of regular features like "Contest for the Gifted and the Damned," "Ask Chatterjee," and "Cook's Corner."

Like the heady scent of coffee and cherry pie, the *Gazette* should serve as a reassuring constant in our community. Please feel free to send your pressing thoughts to: the *Twin Peaks Gazette*, P.O. Box 1804, Pacific Palisades, CA 90272.

Agent Cooper Makes Blacktie's Best-Dressed FBI Agent List

Special Agent Dale Cooper, the FBI agent who recently cracked the Laura Palmer murder case here in Twin Peaks, has made Mr. Blacktie's Ten Best-Dressed FBI Agents list for 1990. Making the list is not easy, as FBI agents tend to dress alike in a conservative, if not completely confidential, style with subtleties not easily detected by the untrained eye. But Mr. Blacktie is a professional critic whose list is exclusive to detectives, both federal and private.

"Agent Cooper always looks fabulous, even his pajamas make an elegant understatement. Cooper's an exceedingly well-dressed and well-spoken public servant," said Mr. Blacktie from his office in Washington, D.C. "He always looks cool and pressed, no matter how messy his work is."

Also making the list this year was Agent Gordon Cole, who had visited Twin Peaks recently. Agent Dennis Bryson, yet another federal investigator in town to fight crime, did not fare so well this year. Agent Bryson, AKA Denise, a cross-dresser, was criticized by Mr. Blacktie for his uneven hemlines and plunging necklines and was unceremoniously put on the Ten Worst-Dressed list.

We were unable to reach Agent Cooper for com-

FBI Agent Dale Cooper

ment and Agent Bryson's comments were unprintable. We reached Agent Cole in Bend, Oregon, who said, "The trout are biting here, too!" which we assume means something relevant in detective lingo.

AUDREY HORNE PHOTO LOOK-ALIKE CONTEST

Do you look like Audrey Horne or just act like her? Do your saddle shoes steam, I mean, do to you really have the look? Send us your best Audrey-like photo and an essay of a hundred words or less explaining how it is you look like you do, or rather, like Ms. Horne does. First prize winner will have his or her photo published in the *Gazette* and receive a $100 gift certificate. Please include your name and Twin Peaks address with photo. Remember, a lot can be done with make-up, lighting and the spirit of deceit.

PHOTO BY PAULA SHIMATSU-U

Town Life

SWITCHBOARD OPERATOR

A casual look through the Twin Peaks telephone directory will reveal its unique organization. Our citizens are listed alphabetically by first name, not last.

How do such things come to be? This oddity finds it's roots in a small village in Ireland, of all places —where Twin Peaks' first phone operator hailed from.

Her name was **McFarley O'Halloran**, which might explain some of her confusion. But those who knew her said it had far more to do with her moody disposition. Once, when asked what her hobby was, she said: "Kicking Cats".

Regardless, **McFarley O'Halloran** came from a long line of rebellious Irish who were contrary just to be so. The old story goes that when **McFarley** arrived at Twin Peaks the only job she could get was switchboard operator. Being kind of heart, authorities gave her the job. "What kind of phone book do you have here?" She asked. When told it was no different than anywhere else she responded, "Well, I'm against it."

So, Twin Peaks is left with its rather odd or eccentric type of listing. But as **Sheriff Truman** says, "It teaches you to remember folks and to keep getting to know them on a first name basis."

He's right! Say you stopped by the Twin Peaks barber shop and had a delightful conversation with a "Gunner". There is hardly a soul who has had their ears lowered to whom Gunner doesn't say. "I'm fourth generation hair." And suppose you'd like to get together with him away from the shop. Well, how simple can it be? Just look under the "G's". It's like **Pete Martell** says. "It gives a whole new meaning to "Let Your Fingers Do the Walking."

Town Life

While she lived, **McFarley** was far better known for her ear-shattering, "WHAT!" which greeted requests for telephone numbers.